Teachers Leading Learning:

Empowering Educators Through Cycles of Instructional Improvement

Copyright © 2025

Bo Ryan

eBook ISBN: 979-8-89795-762-0
Paperback ISBN: 979-8-89795-763-7
Hardcover ISBN: 979-8-89795-764-4

Endorsements

"Bo Ryan's 'Teachers Leading Learning' offers an incredibly practical roadmap for cultivating teacher leadership and enhancing school culture. I was deeply impressed by Ryan's passion, extensive knowledge, and the actionable strategies provided to improve teaching and learning, ultimately benefiting students. I look forward to incorporating these protocols with the teams I work with and empowering more teachers to lead learning. This book is essential reading for any educator or administrator committed to empowering teachers and leading positive change."

David Montemurro, Assistant Principal, Maloney High School

"'Teachers Lead Learning' offers a unique and practical roadmap for school leaders and educators committed to genuine instructional improvement. By integrating a research-backed, five-phase 'Learning Block' cycle with actionable tools and a strong focus on collaborative practice, this book provides the clarity and resources schools need to empower teachers and drive measurable student achievement. A must-have for anyone interested in fostering a culture of continuous learning and impact."

Louis Bronk, Assistant Superintendent for Personnel and Talent Development, Meriden Public Schools

Teachers are overwhelmed by data from multiple sources with no clear system to make sense of it all. Bo Ryan's book finally gives educators what they need—all the essential data tools in one place with a practical framework to turn information into action. This is the streamlined approach to data-driven instruction that teachers have been waiting for.

Dr. Tayarisha Batchelor, Director of Equity and Access/Leadership Consultant, Simsbury Public Schools

Teachers not only lead instruction for students, but they are often called upon to lead instruction for their colleagues. Bo Ryan's book Teachers Leading Learning provides guidance and strategies for the new and experienced teacher to lead learning both within and beyond the classroom.

Paula Talty, Special Assistant to the Provost, Central Connecticut State University

Teachers Leading Teachers is a game-changing book. Providing this tool for teachers supports them in taking charge of their learning. Bo Ryan establishes a structure for the beginning, middle, and end of the year learning cycles. This framework is flexible in that any professional learning committee can apply the process and achieve success. Bo's teacher-friendly, winning formula puts faculty in the driver's seat with practical steps to enhance planning, instruction, and assessment throughout the course of the school year.

Dr. John W. Barile, Sr., Dean - School of Education, Central Connecticut State University

Once again, Bo Ryan hits it out of the park with the exceptional, practical, and applicable addition to his catalog of books. Readers will not only learn of the Five Phases of Teaching and Learning. They will have the opportunity to authentically apply their reading and their learning.

Dr. John D. Ewald, Superintendent of Schools-Retired, Principal-Retired, Solution Tree PLC at Work, RTI at Work, Priority Schools Associate

Teachers Leading Learning is an outstanding, research-based, and equity-focused guide designed to help any educator accelerate learning for all students. Each of the steps of improvement are clear to follow, can be integrated into any instructional improvement plan or framework, and provides the reader with strategies to grow teacher leadership, learning, and expertise within any building. This is a must-have for any teacher, leader, or administrator who is driven to guarantee all students learn at high levels based on the collaborative actions of highly focused teaching teams.

Dr. David Huber, Principal, *Charles Wright Elementary School*, Wethersfield, CT.

Teachers Leading Learning 2025 is more than a book; it's a roadmap for how schools should function when teacher leadership, professional growth, and student learning are truly prioritized. Bo Ryan hands educators a complete, year-long system that turns professional development into meaningful, teacher-led transformation. This isn't theory or fluff; it's a clear structure built for impact, ownership, and sustained growth. The brilliance of this work is in its balance. It's both bold and practical. Visionary and usable. It challenges the status quo without overwhelming the reader. And at every step, it reminds us of a powerful truth: when teachers lead the learning, students win. If you're serious about building a school culture where reflection, collaboration, and instructional excellence are the norm, not the exception, this is the tool you've been waiting for. I couldn't recommend it more.

Chris Jones, Principal and Author, Whitman-Hanson Regional High School

Arranging learning into blocks of time for teams of teachers to move through the five cycles of instructional planning works! It empowers teachers to be the lead learners. It enhances collective teacher efficacy because there is a consistent measurement of learning and a planful celebration of growth. It provides time for students who need more support to have planful small group instruction. Learning blocks build momentum for teams of teachers to know their efforts are working AND meet the needs of all students!

Brendan Hines, Special Education Supervisor,
Capital Region Education Council

Table of Contents

Introduction and Overview:

About the Author:

Bo Ryan is principal of the Ana Grace Academy of the Arts Middle Magnet School in Bloomfield, Connecticut. He is passionate about building and sustaining professional learning communities (PLCs), creating high-performing teams, and transforming school culture. He is also passionate about student learning, especially in the area of literacy, and has created summer programs, after-school programs, intervention programs, and instructional programs, all focused on improving literacy. Bo teaches a literacy class to the most in-need learners. He has led two different schools to Model PLC at Work® certification: Woodside Intermediate School in 2012 and Greater Hartford Academy of the Arts Middle School in 2016, just four years after it opened. In addition, he led Ana Grace Middle School to High Reliability Schools Level 4 Status just 2 years after the entire school moved into a new building. Bo has worked in education since 1994, having served as a teacher, coach, director, adjunct professor, and principal. He started his career in education as a graduate assistant football coach for Syracuse University, coaching in two bowl games. Bo started his teaching career at John C. Clark Elementary School in Hartford, Connecticut, where he was recognized as the city's Teacher and Educator of the Year. During his time there, Bo created various before- and after-school programs for hundreds of students a year. In the summers, he directed a camp called the National Youth Sports Program, which served over 500 children in the city. The program was named the nation's most improved camp a year after Bo took over leadership. Bo also instructed a graduate class on PLCs and interventions as an adjunct professor at the University of Saint Joseph in Hartford, Connecticut.

Bo wrote *The Brilliance in the Building: Effecting Change in Urban Schools With the PLC at Work Process*, a collection of all his experience teaching and learning in urban schools over the last 20 years. His passion for writing this book arose from his incredible experiences growing up in an urban neighborhood. The book was recognized by the International Book Awards as book of the year, and he was named a finalist for author of the year. The book is also a part of Solution Tree's Acceleration Toolkit. Bo's articles "Learning by Doing: The Arts Middle Way" and "Effecting Change in Urban Schools With the PLC Process" are published in *AllThingsPLC Magazine*. Bo has a chapter in each Transforming School Culture Anthology, *Culture Keepers,* and *Culture Champions..* Currently, Alexander McNeese and Bo are finalizing the book, *Transforming School Culture*. Bo has been on the following shows:

- Conversation with Brian Podcast

- Brilliance in the Building ED Webinar

- SEEING to Lead Podcast

- Learning Unboxed with Annalies Corbin

- Charting New Paths in PreK-12 Education (Coming in August)

Bo is certified with Solution Tree in PLCs, Response to Intervention (RTI), Transforming School Culture, and Priority Schools in a PLC at Work. In addition, he is certified with Marzano in High Reliability Schools and The New Art and Science of Teaching. He has worked with schools across the United States. Lastly, he is also trained to coach and certify others for High Reliability Teachers and High Reliability Schools. He earned undergraduate degrees from Western Connecticut State University, a master's degree from Syracuse University, and a sixth-year degree from Southern Connecticut State University.

Resources from the book

Staff can use the electronic version of this book or do the work in the hard copy.

Purpose of the Book

I have dedicated over 30 years to the field of education and have spent the past 25 years developing this book, beginning with my early career as a physical education teacher in Hartford, Connecticut. At that time, I was given no curriculum, guidance, or framework for lesson delivery or assessments. As a new teacher with no curriculum or guidance, I was honestly scrambling and worried I wasn't giving my students what they deserved. That experience taught me that even teachers who care deeply need solid support systems to really make a difference. In response, I immersed myself in studying state and national standards and began designing structured learning blocks aligned with those expectations. My students engaged not only in physical education activities but also explored careers in sports, studied the history of various games, and participated in discussions on teamwork, fitness, and the broader impact of sports on society.

As my career progressed and I transitioned into school leadership, I committed myself to reading extensively and refining my practice to support and develop effective teaching across classrooms. My goal has always been to help educators make the most of every instructional minute to support high levels of student learning. The instructional tools featured in this book have been tested, refined, and successfully implemented over the course of two decades in classrooms ranging from Pre-K to high school. Over my 30 years, I've used these tools in urban districts like Hartford, where I started, and later in suburban settings. What I learned is that while the neighborhoods look different, teachers everywhere need the same kind of systematic support to help kids succeed. I am constantly learning myself - whether it's preparing a presentation, teaching a reading class, or coaching teachers - because I know that if I stop growing, I can't help other teachers grow either.

Throughout my career, I've had the privilege of working alongside exceptional educators. However, the educational landscape is shifting. Schools are facing increasing challenges, including staffing shortages, high rates of absenteeism, and gaps in staff preparedness. This book is designed to support building leaders who need practical tools to guide professional learning and maximize instructional impact. This book could guide an entire year of professional development and learning for all staff in the building. The tools in this book could jumpstart any school on its path to creating a Professional Learning Community, a High-Reliability School, and a school focused on Response to Intervention. Also, the book was intentionally made to be short in order to give quick directions and give staff the time to lead the work. No more long staff meetings or meaningless professional development. This book can help our building leaders all over the world! It also serves as a valuable resource for non-certified staff and substitute teachers who may need clarity on effective teaching practices and assessment strategies. New teachers will find these tools especially helpful in establishing a strong foundation, while veteran educators will appreciate how these resources elevate their practice and empower them to drive their own professional growth. In today's fast-paced environment, teachers often lack the time to read lengthy books on pedagogy, design their own tools, and train others to use them. The tools in this book work best when done in collaborative teams, but are also very powerful when done with teachers who are singletons in their school. All staff can use this book, including administration, to focus the entire staff on learning. As both an educator and a parent, I understand that anxious feeling of wondering whether a child's learning time is truly being used well. That dual perspective drives me to ensure that every moment in the classroom counts.

This book introduces a streamlined, five-phase instructional improvement cycle: **Plan, Instruct, Measure Learning, Data Action,** and **Professional Learning**. Each phase is thoughtfully aligned to support continuous growth, instructional clarity, and student achievement. The professional learning component centers on teacher choice and autonomy. Instructional coaches will find this model particularly valuable as a way to guide conversations and practices toward student-centered, high-impact teaching. There are not many books that have these 5 phases in one book.

This book isn't just about my professional experience - it's personal, for 2 reasons. One, as a child, I did not focus on academics as I needed to during my middle and high school years. During middle school, I was failing most of my classes and also getting in trouble in the neighborhood. My mother changed her work hours as an emergency nurse from the day shift to the overnight shift in order to visit the school to check on me. She also created a "Scared Straight" Program with the local police to make sure that I understood the ramifications for breaking the law and for being around others who were breaking the law. Reason two: my father sent me to prep school in May of my senior year in high school because I did not have any options, and it saved my life. I learned how powerful a team of adults can be in the life of a child. I finished first in my class at Cushing Academy Prep School. My second reason, I wanted to help all of the amazing teachers lead their learning, no matter the conditions.   It comes from remembering my own early struggles as a teacher and my ongoing commitment as a parent and lifelong learner to make sure every educator has what they need to succeed.

Book Overview:

Part 1: The first section of this book gives a few tools to allow teachers to lead the learning in the building and create a systematic culture focused on learning. The practices in this book are used to guide collaborative teams teaching the same subject. The tools are also just as effective for individual subject teachers to use to impact their learning and student learning. All teachers benefit from studying the curriculum, planning a block of time, teaching at a high level, measuring learning with assessments, reflecting on the data to change practice, and other professional development choices to help improve in the process. The more teachers plan, especially when planning in collaborative teams, the more they will improve their practice.

Part 2: This section focuses on cycles of planning, instruction, measuring learning, data action, and professional learning. In this part, there are 4 sections of materials, all of the same type. All of the materials are easy to follow for teams with clear directions on how to do the work. The first tool is used for planning out the standards for the entire year. The learning blocks, each phase, align with the curriculum of your district or school. Teams must take the time to read and reflect on the curriculum, but also have the power to make slight revisions based on student learning. After planning the instructional block, teachers set learning goals for the cycle and reflect on their practice. During this time, they also create, administer, and score common formative assessments, then analyze the results to take meaningful Data Action.

All of the tools in this section align with research-based best practices in education. Teachers could write in this book, and this benefits them to refer back to previous sections during the course of the year. Teachers will improve their practice every time they complete a cycle of learning!

Part 3: This section has tools that staff can use at the end-of-year professional learning sessions.

Part 1: Teachers Leading Learning at the Beginning of the Year

All of these tools can be used by teachers and staff during their back-to-school professional development days.

Everyone is Accountable: Start Here!

Purpose: The purpose of this tool is for leaders in the building to review the criteria for creating a system focused on learning. We cannot tell staff to go work in teams without giving time embedded in the work day beyond the prep, ensuring the success of the teams, and offering coaching to teams who need extra help. Every teacher can lead this process.

Directions: Leaders read the key indicators and mark either yes, we have that practice, or no, we do not have the practice. The indicators below must all be met before allowing the Teachers to Lead Learning.

Key Indicators	Yes/No
Staff are clear on the mission of the school: student learning.	
Staff understand the school-wide focus on collaboration and professional learning.	
Leaders must review the tools in this book with the staff in order to make sure everyone is on the same page.	
Staff are organized in meaningful teams (grade-level, subject-specific, and vertical).	
Special Education Teachers must be in grade-level meetings and collaborate with the team.	
Teams are provided time to collaborate beyond the prep on a daily/weekly basis.	
Teams are all focused on a collective vision of improving student learning.	
Teams are all set up to ensure their success with resources, time, and tools.	
Teacher leadership will monitor the work of teams, provide direction and support, and help coach the teams.	
Teams share short-term wins and celebrate their work on a regular basis.	

Coaching is offered to support teams who need a little extra help and support.	
School-based leadership understands that this resource gives teachers flexibility to lead their professional learning during assigned days.	
The school has a plan to give all students more time and support for their learning during the school day.	
Plan of action for indicators not yet met	

Creating Brilliant Teams: Team Norms

Purpose: The purpose of this tool is to make sure that everyone understands the expectations of the behavior of adults in team meetings.

Directions: Teams review the document below and create their own norms. Norms must be reviewed before every meeting and sometimes during the meeting.

Definition of Norms: behaviors that the team expects members to adhere to during a meeting.
How to use Norms: review at the beginning and end of meetings
Example of Norms: • We will maximize time • We will be engaged • We will be prepared for every meeting • We will learn from each other
Our Norms
How we plan to solve-problems as a team

Creating Brilliant Teams: Team Roles

<u>Purpose:</u> The purpose of this tool is to make sure that everyone understands their role during the meeting.

<u>Directions:</u> Teams review the document below and assign roles before every meeting.

Role	Description
Facilitator	Listens attentively to all members, summarizes discussions when needed, reminds the group of the meeting's objectives and established guidelines, steers the meeting in accordance with protocols, generates outcomes, observes group interactions, ensures that every participant is heard, interrupts side conversations, redirects discussions, and, above all, appreciates the team process.
Recorder or Note-taker	Documents big ideas of the meeting without adding opinions, checks with participants as needed to ensure accurate recording, distributes notes to the team and principal, and archives all notes in an agreed-upon location.
Time Keeper	Follows time frames, informs the group of time either verbally or nonverbally, and works with the facilitator to negotiate time frames.
Engaged Participant	Engages in the work, listens, questions, contributes, commits, believes he or she can make an impact, and plans to take collective action.

Revised from Ryan, B. (2023). *Brilliance in the building: effecting change in urban schools with the PLC at Work process*. Bloomington, IN: Solution Tree Press.

Creating Brilliant Teams: Team Expectations

<u>Purpose:</u> The purpose of this tool is to make sure that everyone understands the expectations of the team.

<u>Directions</u>: Teams review the document below when needed by team leaders.

- As a team, the primary focus of our meetings will be on continuously improving the learning of all of our students and each other.   The daily focus will be instruction and student results.

- As a team, we will make all students, regardless of their class or grade, the concern of everyone. We will move from the culture of "my" students to "our" students. We will take collective responsibility for ALL students!

- As a team, we will anticipate potential questions, complex issues, and problems that have a huge impact on student learning and collectively seek the best ways to respond.

- As a team, we will openly share learning data, always seeking to help and support each other, as well as learn from each other, in order to continuously improve our practice.

- As a team, we will make decisions by consensus only after listening to all points of view.

- As a team, if we didn't say it in the meeting, we will not say it in the parking lot.

Ensure Access for ALL with ACTIONS

<u>Purpose:</u> The purpose of this tool is to ensure that all students have access to grade-level curriculum during core, classroom instruction.

<u>Directions:</u> This is a great tool to share with teams and the entirety of the staff in order to ensure that all students have access to grade-level curriculum on a daily basis. Teams read each adult action below and check if they can collectively commit to the adult action.

Adult Actions	Collective Commitment
Identify the priority standards from the curriculum - study the curriculum.	
Maximize time in the classrooms by limiting interruptions.	
Dedicate a sufficient amount of time in the master schedule for teaching the priority standards.	
Create classroom assignments that align with the grade-level standard.	
Ensure access for all students in every classroom to grade-level assignments.	
Ensure all students and staff are clear on the success criteria, exemplary work, worked examples, and mastery models.	
Eliminate below-grade level tracks in the school.	
Eliminate below-grade-level tracks in the classroom.	
Ensure students are not to be removed from core classroom instruction unless part of an IEP.	

Guarantee all students receive grade-level curriculum as part of their instruction.	
Dismiss students on time to arrive at class on time.	
Measure student learning of the guaranteed and viable curriculum with common formative assessments created by teachers with immediate flex time to review and reteach.	
Ensure programs and practices are in place to help students meet individual achievement goals when data indicate extra support is needed.	
Analyze data to regularly monitor progress toward school achievement goals and goals for individual students.	

Revised from: Simms, J. (2024). The marzano synthesis: A collected guide to what works in K-12 Education. Bloomington, IN: Solution Tree Press. Buffum, A., Mattos, M., & Malone, J. (2018). *Taking action: A handbook for RTI at Work*. Bloomington, IN: Solution Tree Press.Buffum, A., M

Our Current Reality

<u>Purpose:</u> The goal is to give all stakeholders in the school shared knowledge of the current data picture of the school on a yearly basis, at the start of the school year. All staff members in the building must be allowed to participate in the review of this document.

<u>Directions:</u> Staff members complete the tool before the staff meeting. At the start of the meeting, the team reviews norms for the meeting and the core values. Staff members study the data individually and list facts and thoughts. Groups discuss each other's responses and share with the entire staff. The entire staff then discusses and creates a plan of action.

Demographic Data				
Indicator	**Year**	**Year**	**Year**	**Facts about our Data**
Percent free and reduced lunch				
Percent mobility				
Percent Special Education				
Percent of Two or More Races				
Percent black				

Percent White				
Percent Hispanic				
Percent Chronically absent				

Reflection on the previous year's Staff and Student Attendance Data:

Reflection on the previous year's Academic Data:

Reflection on the previous year's Behavior Data:

Priority Standards Map for Year

Purpose: The purpose of this task is to study the curriculum in its entirety with a subject-specific team or vertical team.

Directions: The leaders study the curriculum, discuss and review the priority standards, select and define essential vocabulary, discuss the length of time needed for students to master, and the cycle in which the standards will be taught. If the staff completed the Flashback Priority Plan from the previous year, then they will have a few particularly difficult priority standards. Leaders can plan more time and specific practices for the standards.

Accountability Log		
Dates Met/Times	**Location Met**	**Staff Present at Meeting**

Greeting/Check-In	Norms Review	Roles	Outcome

If available, study the Flashback Priority Sheet in Section 3.

Priority Standards Map for Year					
Priority Standard	Essential Vocabulary of the Standard	Learning Cycle Taught	Learning Cycle Reinforced	Was this standard a challenge last year?	What will you do differently this year?

Current Reality: Systems of Supports for Learning

Purpose: All students can learn, but some may need more time and support in order to learn. In order to create a systematic and schoolwide focus on learning, schools must reflect on the current reality of the school. A system of more time and support will look different in different schools based on the factors below. The goal is to create a systematic plan to give all students who need it more time and support in learning. All staff will be involved in creating the system of support for all students. All staff members must take this survey in order to build shared knowledge of the current reality of the school. Staff members will all be involved in problem-solving conversations based on the current reality of the school. This is going to help create a collective focus on purpose.

Directions: Staff members will all complete the survey, which will lead to problem-solving conversations.

System of Supports for Learning	
Factors to Consider	**Current Reality**
Student Learning Data	
Use of Priority Standards	
Space for interventions and enrichment	
Resources Available	

Time of the day	
Current Schedule	
District and Union Mandates	
Building Space	
Staff Available	
Transitions	
Cafeteria Coverage	
Duty Coverage	

Reflection and Discussion

Options to Provide More Time and Support	Description
Flex Time	Time during the school day where the teacher does not teach new material but gives students more time and support, or enrichment and extension based on the priority standards taught and assessed in the classroom.
Flex Days	Time is built into the schedule after a common assessment to give the student more time and support, enrichment, and extension in the classroom. Support staff go to the classroom.
Scheduled Time in Schedule	Time embedded in the schedule (30-35 minutes) during the day, where students travel to a classroom for more support, IEP support, enrichment, or extension. This practice includes more staff members and more space. The collaborative teams decide where students need support based on the common formative assessment data.

Combination of time embedded, Flex Time, and Flex Block	Teams use a combination of the 3 practices above.
Action Plan	

Revised from Ryan, B. (2023). Brilliance in the building: Effecting change in urban schools at a PLC at Work. Solution

Plan for More Time and Support

Purpose: The document below is an easy graphic organizer to start the process of giving all students in your school more time and support in their learning during the day.

Directions: The staff meets as a leadership team to plan the block of time that is outside of core instruction. Staff creates a plan for students for the first 23 minutes of the block and a plan for the last 23 minutes. See example below.

Students w/IEP Services and Enrichment Class	**1st 23 Minutes**	
	3 Minutes	Movement Break Students Transition
	2nd 23 Minutes	

Teams meet to discuss the following questions:

1. Which students need more time and support to reach mastery?

2. Which classes do the students need the most time and support with?

3. How many days a week will we offer more time and support?

4. Which students do you need on ___________ days?

5. Which students need extension?

6. Which students need enrichment?

Students w/IEP Services and Enrichment Class	1st 23 Minutes	→ **Math:** Intensive Reinforcement in the Foundational skills for Math focused on data from <u>CFAs</u>, <u>vocabulary</u>, <u>prior knowledge</u>, <u>math reading</u>, and <u>math skills</u> aligned to the standard. Create an assessment to measure learning during this time.
		→ <u>Literacy SPECIFIC! (SS, Science, ELA, MLL)</u> Intensive Reinforcement in the Foundational Literacy Lessons focused on <u>word work</u>, <u>vocabulary</u>, <u>fluency</u>, <u>writing</u>, and <u>comprehension</u>
	3 Minutes	Movement Break Students Transition
	2nd 23 Minutes	→ **Math:** Additional time and support to learn grade-level priority standards and re-engage and reteach grade-level standards after common formative assessment.
		Enrichment Arts
		→ <u>SUBJECT SPECIFIC!</u> ELA, <u>Social Studies, and Science</u>: Additional time and support to learn grade-level priority standards and re-engage and reteach grade-level standards after common formative assessments for the subject or daily lessons.

Flex Time Expectations

Purpose: Time used after every common formative assessment to reteach using different strategies and extend learning aligned to the grade-level priority standards.

Directions: Classrooms with below 80% of class at mastery or above must utilize flex time as a collaborative team or singleton. All students stay in the classroom with no pull-out services.

Flex Time Strategies	
Student Self-Grading	Students self-grade their assessments using success criteria.
Retakes and Reteaching	The teacher allows students to correct mistakes and resubmit their assessments. Teachers must use different strategies when reteaching the material to the students.
Whole Class Review	The teacher reviews the assessment with the entire class.
Students below Mastery	Teacher reviews and reteaches prerequisite skills and success criteria for mastery.
Students above Mastery	The teacher gives an assignment to push students' thinking beyond grade level.
Collaborative Teams	Teams can meet to divide students into the different classrooms. For example, the math teacher takes the mastery or higher group, and the other math teacher takes the "Not Yet" Group.

Introduction to Learning Blocks: Ensuring Effective Instruction in Every Classroom

Purpose: The purpose is to introduce the educator to the cycle of the learning process.

Directions: Teams read, review, and reflect on the process.

❖ Learning Blocks are the clear vision as to how instruction should be addressed in the school. They are blocks of time focused on planning, instruction, assessing, data action, and professional development. Cycles consist of multiple learning blocks.

❖ Support is provided to teachers to continually enhance their pedagogical skills through the Learning Block Process.

❖ The Learning Block Practices of planning, assessing, high-quality instruction, data action, and professional learning will be monitored.

❖ Teachers are provided with time during the day for job-embedded professional development that is directly related to the Learning Block Process.

❖ Teachers can set goals, see below, to monitor the growth of the students in their classrooms. SMART goals are Specific, Measurable, Attainable, Relevant, and Timely. Teams and teachers should set SMART goals before each learning block.

SMART GOAL	The percentage of students showing growth during each learning cycle will increase from __________ to ___________ as measured by common formative assessments at the end of the block.

Learning Blocks Overview

Learning blocks consist of a systematic approach involving five phases: planning, teaching, assessment, data actions, and professional learning. These are designated periods where educators collaborate to identify key standards, break them down into specific learning targets, develop learning or proficiency scales, establish success criteria, and create, implement, and score common formative assessments or CFAs. Teachers work individually if a singleton or in a team to reflect on the data and take action to improve student learning. The assessments are given at the beginning of the block, Pre-CFA, the middle of the block, Mid-CFA, and at the end of the block, or End-CFA. The data collected is then analyzed to inform subsequent actions and professional learning for teams and individuals.

Rather than waiting for evidence to determine student learning, we proactively assess, collaborate, and implement strategies to support student success. The structured steps within the learning block process are designed to ensure that all students achieve high levels of learning, resulting in a curriculum that is both guaranteed and viable. This approach fosters an equitable learning environment by providing all students access to the core curriculum. In order to ensure effective instruction in all classrooms, teachers must constantly observe, read, discuss, and reflect on effective instruction. Common formative assessments serve not only to measure student learning but also to verify that teachers are effectively delivering the guaranteed and viable curriculum. Educators utilize assessment data to reflect on their teaching methods and formulate action plans for both students who struggle and those who succeed.

Following the common formative assessment, if students are not grasping the material, teachers should pause and use flex time to offer additional support and preparation for all students. If learning challenges persist during the learning block, another common formative assessment should be administered to all students, followed by team collaboration and the use of another Flex Block to provide further assistance. The significance of this process cannot be overstated. The goal is to measure student learning.

Teachers will engage in four cycles of learning blocks that consist of planning, teaching, administering common formative assessments, meeting in data teams to take action, and selected professional development. Each team is required to conduct both pre and post assessments, with the flexibility to choose their dates. All subjects at all grades can participate.

Cycle	Dates
Learning Block 1	
Learning Block 2	
Learning Block 3	
Learning Block 4	

The table below defines all of the key vocabulary needed to be able to access the material in this book.

Learning Blocks	
Learning Block Term	Definition
Learning Block	Designated periods where educators collaborate or work individually, if a singleton teacher, to identify key standards, break them down into specific learning targets, develop learning or proficiency scales, establish success criteria, create, implement, and score common formative assessments, take data action, and select professional learning based on the data.
Cycles of Learning Blocks	Multiple learning blocks.
Common Formative Assessment	A type of assessment created by teams to measure the learning of all the students.
Guaranteed and Viable Curriculum	Teachers work together to ensure that all students have access to the same grade-level curriculum with time to learn the material, no matter the teacher.
Singleton	Teachers who are the only ones teaching the subject.
Mastery Models, Exemplary Work, or Worked Examples	Student or teacher work that demonstrates mastery of the grade-level learning target.
Flex Time	More time and support for all students to learn grade-level material after an assessment.
Prior to Learning Block CFA	A pre-assessment is given at the beginning of the block to measure prerequisite skills.

Prior-to-Learning Block Data Team	Teams convene to chart, discuss, and analyze pre-assessment data and collaboratively develop a plan for instruction, the pacing of the block, and the flex blocks.
Flex Prior-to-Learning Block	Students engage in self-assessment and participate in the evaluation process. Teachers concentrate on teaching vocabulary for the unit and the prerequisite skills aligned to the priority standards, using the data to drive instruction. Flex time should be utilized if 80% of the students did not reach mastery.
High-Quality Instruction	Instruction focuses on grade-level priority standards. Teachers leverage a proficiency scale as an instructional resource to ensure a guaranteed and viable curriculum, which supports high-impact strategies such as clarity in teaching, feedback, formative assessment, questioning, and student grading. All students must have access to the priority standards taught during core instruction.
Mid-CFA	During the unit assessment to measure learning is measured over the course of 5-8 days.
Mid-Block Data Team	Teams meet to analyze data from the mid-unit CFA, creating plans for flex blocks tailored to students who have mastered the material and those who have not.
Flex During Block	Students self-grade and engage in the assessment process. Teachers re-engage students in their learning, allowing for retakes and reviews. Flex time must be utilized if 80% of students do not achieve mastery.
End-of-Learning Block CFA	A common formative assessment at the end of the unit that evaluates learning across the entire unit

End-of-Learning Unit Block Data Team	The team meets to review overall data for growth, breaking down learning targets by mastery and student performance. They develop a plan for instruction, flex time, and college preparation, with data guiding the allocation of flex days.
Flex End-of-Learning Block	Students self-grade, track their progress, and participate in the assessment process. Teachers re-teach learning targets that were not mastered and enhance learning for those who have achieved mastery. Flex time must be utilized if 80% of students do not reach mastery.
Celebrate	Recognize and celebrate the achievements of both students and staff.
Professional Learning	Staff must always be working to improve their practice. Teachers must have the option, at times, to select the professional learning and choose to work either independently, with others, or to teach others.

The figure below shows a visual representation of the Learning Block Process. It starts with a pre-assessment, flex time to pre-teach critical vocabulary and prerequisite skills, high-quality instruction, and mid-block assessment with flex time, and the end of the block common formative assessment with flex time. All students must have the opportunity for more time and support during the flex time, which focuses on student learning.

Learning Blocks

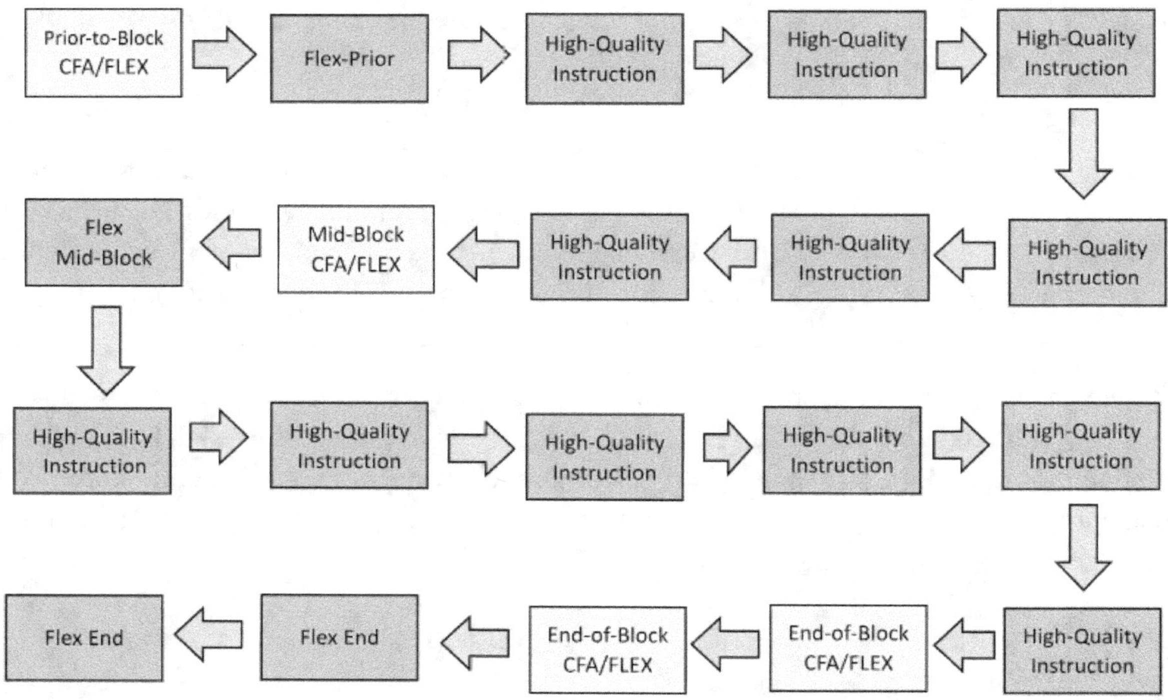

Learning Blocks: Essential Actions

- Examine, review, and discuss the grade-level curriculum for the specific subject.

- Complete the planning process with your subject-specific team. Singleton teachers should share insights with their vertical teams. This step involves documenting the curriculum in writing.

- Plan for the entire cycle and take time to reflect on your work throughout this period.

- Display a Proficiency Scale in your classroom that includes information from the Learning Block Plan. This takes the team meeting to the classroom. It must be mandatory for every staff member to have a proficiency scale visible in their classroom for student use.

- Create, administer, and evaluate common formative assessments (CFA) at the beginning, middle, and end of the learning block. Utilize the provided link for CFA creation.

- Utilize Flex Time after every CFA administered by all staff members.

- Conduct pre-block common assessments to evaluate prior knowledge and prerequisite skills. Mid-block assessments should gauge student learning at the halfway point.

- Collaborate with your specific team at the conclusion of your learning block for the quarter.

- Record professional learning throughout the learning block cycle.

- Focus on improving as an instructional leader in the classroom.

- Ensure your professional learning is aligned with student outcomes.

Part 2: Teachers Leading the Learning During the Year

All of these tools can be used by teachers and staff during the school year during their professional development time.

Learning Block 1

Dates	
SMART Goal	

Phase 1: Planning

Ensure a Guaranteed and Viable Curriculum

8 Action Steps for a successful learning plan meeting:

Step 1: Begin by greeting one another, conducting a check-in, revisiting established norms, and discussing desired outcomes.

Step 2: Examine the curriculum in detail.

Step 3: Engage in discussions to review and prioritize standards.

Step 4: Develop proficiency scales for sharing within the classroom.

Step 5: Outline the pacing for the unit.

Step 6: Formulate an instructional plan.

Step 7: Plan for additional time and support.

Step 8: Collaboratively planning a block of time is exemplary professional learning. In addition, organize your professional development to align with the planning.

Learning Plan

Purpose: Allow staff members to plan to create a guaranteed and viable curriculum, which ensures that all students have access to the curriculum and the time to learn it. Educational researcher and author Dr. Robert Marzano states that it is the number one factor impacting student learning.

Directions: The learning plan is for all certified teachers in the school in all grade levels: grade-level teams, subject-specific teams, singleton teachers, and humanities teachers. Staff use the allotted time during the day to study and take notes on the curriculum, review priority standards, create mastery models of expected student work, create a pacing guide, and create an instructional plan. This is also a tool that can be used by coaches to guide teachers and offer support. The teacher leads this process.

Step 1: Greetings

Accountability Log		
Dates Met/Times	**Location Met**	**Staff Present at Meeting**

Greeting/Check-In	Norms Review	Roles	Outcome

Step 2: Curriculum

Study the Curriculum Materials and Take Notes

Study the Curriculum Materials and Take Notes

Step 3: Discuss and Review Priority Standards

<table>
<tr><td colspan="2">List Priority Standards for Cycle of Learning with GUARANTEED Vocabulary that must be taught (post in room)</td></tr>
<tr><td>Priority Standards</td><td>Guaranteed Vocabulary</td></tr>
<tr><td></td><td></td></tr>
<tr><td colspan="2">Learning Targets Created from the Standard(s)</td></tr>
</table>

Process for Creating Proficiency Scales to ensure guaranteed and viable curriculum:

1. Write the learning target for mastery of standards
2. Write success criteria for mastery: what does good work look like with mastery models
3. Determine vocabulary, teach vocabulary simpler procedures, and prerequisite content
4. Discuss thinking beyond mastery with examples of exceeding
5. Discuss scaffolds for each target and teaching tips

Step 4: Create Learning Progression and Proficiency Scales

Learning Target	Approaching Standard Prerequisite Skills Guaranteed Vocabulary	Mastery of Standard w/Success Criteria	Exceeding Standard Thinking beyond mastery	Scaffolds for the Learning Targets & Teaching Tips for Exceeding Assignments
LT1				
Mastery Model, Exemplary, or Worked Example of Learning Target				
LT2				

Mastery Model, Exemplary, or Worked Example of Learning Target				
LT3				
Mastery Model, Exemplary, or Worked Example of Learning Target				
LT4				

Mastery Model, Exemplary, or Worked Example of Learning Target

Step 5: Create Pacing for the Block

- **Examine** the curriculum, district assessment calendar, and overall district calendar.

- **Outline the schedule** for teaching learning targets, conducting common formative assessments, and allocating time for data monitoring and reflection.

- **Designate specific days** for teaching particular standards and strategize on how to assess learning through common formative assessments.

- **Identify anticipated team meeting days** and ensure alignment of professional development with these plans: review and develop the learning cycle plan, create and implement common formative assessments, analyze and reflect on the data, and formulate a data-driven action plan.

- **This collaborative strategy must be mutually agreed upon** and adhered to by the team. If they cannot, they follow the curriculum as closely as possible or ask an instructional coach for additional support and expertise.

Bo Ryan

| Focus: | Number of Days: |
| | |

Pacing of Cycle from ____________ to ____________

Monday	Tuesday	Wednesday	Thursday	Friday

Step 6: Create an Instructional Plan

<table>
<tr><td colspan="2" align="center">Instructional Plan</td></tr>
<tr><td colspan="2">

- How will you ensure <u>ALL</u> students have access to grade-level assignments?

- How will your team enrich and extend the learning of students beyond mastery?

- What teaching practices work best for this specific priority standard?

- Plan small-group instruction and/or conferences for students not at mastery.

Small Group Math   Small Group Literacy

</td></tr>
<tr><td colspan="2">

</td></tr>
</table>

Step 7: Create a Plan for More Time and Support:

Systematic Plan for More Time and Support		
Focus	Teaching Plan	Monitor Progress
More Time and Support on grade-level priority standards		
More time and Support on Prerequisite Skills are needed to master grade-level standards		
Fluency Repeated Reading Program		
Enrichment		
IEP Plans		

Arts	42	
Action Plan		

Revised from Ryan, B (2023). Brilliance in the building: Effecting change in urban schools using the PLC process. Solution tree.

Phase 2: Measuring Learning

Creating, Administering, and Scoring Common Formative Assessments

6 steps for having a successful meeting about common formative assessments:

Step 1: Begin by greeting one another, conducting a check-in, revisiting established norms, and discussing desired outcomes.

Step 2: Examine the criteria for developing common formative assessments (CFAs)

Step 3: Develop a CFA(s).

Step 4: Consider the reliability and validity of the CFA.

Step 5: Review, reflect, and agree on shared commitments.

Step 6: Creating common formative assessments is considered exemplary professional learning. In addition, organize a professional learning plan aligned to assessments.

Measuring Learning with Common Formative Assessments

Purpose: The purpose of the grade-level common formative assessment is to measure student learning of the guaranteed and viable curriculum. This tool gives all stakeholders shared knowledge of how to create a reliable and valid common formative assessment. The entire staff can use this in order to create common formative assessments.

Directions: Review the criteria below to support your creation of common formative assessments or performance assessments.

Step 1: Greetings

Accountability Log		
Dates Met/Times	**Location Met**	**Staff Present**

Greeting/Check-In	Norms Review	Roles	Outcome

Step 2: Examine the criteria for developing common formative assessments (CFAs)

Check	Success Criteria for an Exemplary Common Formative Assessment
	The team/teacher discusses and identifies priority standard (s) to be measured.
	The team/teacher writes the assessment around a priority standard.
	The team/teacher evaluates the depth of knowledge level (DOK) of the target(s), selects the best strategy for assessing the target (selected response, constructed response, a combination, or performance task), and aligns the assessment to the rigor of the standard.
	The team/teacher creates the assessment items that match the level of thinking of the target (determine DOK level and align to the level of demand of the question).
	The team/teacher agrees on what mastery will look like for the priority standards and the overall assessment with clear success criteria.
	The team/teacher identifies the academic language and vocabulary that need to be targeted.
	The team ensures the CFA meets the criteria: 1- 2 constructed responses, 2-4 selected responses, or a combination of both per assessment.
	The team/teacher creates an assessment that is neat, organized, and easy to read with adequate space to write and solve problems. The directions and questions are clearly written. The learning target(s) are written on the assessment.
	The team/teacher creates an assessment that is quick to administer, appropriate for the time allotted, and easy to score.

	The students must be a part of the assessment process: clarity on mastery of the standard, review of the assessment, opportunity to retake, and time in the schedule for flex time for reteaching from the teacher. Students set goals and celebrate growth.

Success Criteria for an Exemplary Performance Assessment	
	The team/teacher determines the focus of the performance assessment.
	The team/teacher makes sure the assessment aligns with the priority standard.
	The team/teacher is clear about what the students must demonstrate for mastery.
	The team/teacher creates success criteria to describe the expectations of mastery.
	The team/teacher assesses the students by observation or examining a product.
	The team/teacher will share examples of the performance assessment.

Revised from Ryan, B (2023). Brilliance in the building: Effecting change in urban schools using the PLC process. Solution tree.

Step 3: Develop a CFA.

<u>Common Formative Assessment Framework Model</u>

<u>Student Name:</u>		Date:	Grade:
<u>Name of CFA:</u>			
<u>Standard:</u>			
<u>Precise Directions for CFA</u>:			
<u>Questions Aligned to LT</u>			

Review the Learning Plan and Share Links of your Common Formative Assessments for this Cycle			
Pre-CFA	Mid-CFA	Additional CFA	End-CFA

Step 4: Review Common Formative Assessments and Formative Assessments for Reliability and Validity

The essence of assessments lies in ensuring they are both reliable and valid.

- **Validity:** This refers to the extent to which an assessment accurately measures what the team believes students should have learned, ensuring alignment with instructional goals.

- **Reliability:** This indicates that students who demonstrate understanding of the concepts have genuinely grasped them.

Three Intentional Steps for Developing Valid and Reliable Assessments:

1. Identify the learning target.

2. Determine the level of rigor of the target.

3. Decide on the types and quantity of items for the assessment.

Evaluating the Quality of an Assessment

Is it VALID?

We have pinpointed specific learning targets.

We have established the rigor level for each target.

The assessment items correspond to the cognitive demands of the learning targets.

Is it RELIABLE?

We utilized a sufficient number of questions to ensure reliability.

The team has reached a consensus on the criteria for mastery.

The reading levels of the questions do not hinder the assessment.

Adapted from the work of Ainsworth, Bailey, Erkens, Ferriter, Jakicic, Kramer, Schuhl, Kanold, Barnes, Toncheff, Marzano, Buffum, Malone, Strong, Vagle, Marzano CEU Course on Formative Assessments, Global PD videos, Stronge and Associates, and Global PD Mini-Course on CFA

Step 5: Review, reflect, and agree on shared commitments.

Common Formative Assessment Team Commitments	
Yes, I commit	**Team Member Commitments**
	We agree that the common formative assessment measures grade-level learning for all students.
	We agree that the common formative assessment meets the success criteria listed on page —
	We agree that the common formative assessment created is both reliable and viable.
	We agree to implement the assessment on the same date and time. Date of CFA: Times:
	We agree to give the same directions to our students before the CFA.
	We agree to allow the following amount of time for the assessment:
	We agree to supply the following materials for the students:
	We agree that all students will take the CFA in the classroom.
	We agree on the following scoring plan for the CFA________________ with mastery level __________________ .

	We agree to collaboratively score the assessment with our team on the following dates ___________________ in the following location_______________.
	We agree or disagree to allow students to self-grade their assessments.
	We agree that all students have the opportunity to retake the assessment.
	We agree to the following timeline of the common formative assessments: • Assessment Development: • Administration of the CFA Window: • Date to Collaboratively Score: • Scoring Completion: • Data Action Meeting: • Flex Time on the following day: • Instructional Adjustments Implemented:

Phase 3: Classroom Instruction

Ensuring High Quality Instruction in all Classrooms

6 Action Steps for a successful meeting focused on instruction:

Step 1: Begin by greeting one another, conducting a check-in, revisiting established norms, and discussing desired outcomes.

Step 2: Read, reflect, and review the Teacher Framework multiple times.

Step 3: Reflect on and discuss areas for improvement in your teaching practices using the Teacher Framework Success Criteria.

Step 4: Create and display the proficiency scales in your classroom, observe exemplary scales in other classrooms, and consult the Proficiency Scales guide.

Step 5: Engage in instructional rounds by visiting other classrooms to enhance your instructional methods.

Step 6: Ensuring high-quality instruction on a daily basis by creating instructional action plans and using proficiency scales is quality professional learning. In addition, organize your professional development to align with improving instruction.

Ensuring Effective Instruction in Every Classroom

<u>Purpose:</u> This section is designed for staff to meet as teams or individually to reflect on and improve classroom instruction. The goal is for every staff member to embrace continuous growth as a relentless learner and effective teacher.

<u>Directions:</u> Teachers read and reread the framework, then take notes in *the Reflection on Teaching section*. Teachers consider their current level of instruction, identify an area for growth, and create an action plan to improve your practice.

This phase draws heavily on the work of Robert Marzano's New Art and Science of Teaching and the PLC Framework from Solution Tree - Bo Ryan

Step 1: Greetings

Accountability Log		
Dates Met/Times	**Location Met**	**Staff Present at Meeting**

Greeting/Check-In	Norms Review	Roles	Outcome

Step 2: Read, reflect, and review the Teacher Framework multiple times.

Classroom Learning Environment	Got It!	Possible Area of Focus
Classroom Arrangement: The classroom is neat, safe, and well-organized.		
Standard Wall: The standards wall has the learning targets posted for the month written as student friendly learning goals with clear expectations for grade-level work.		
Do-Now: A brief activity is posted on standard wall or power point.		
Behavior Expectations: Behavior expectations are posted in the room.		
Word Walls: The wall shares high frequency words, words commonly misspelled in students' work, and academic vocabulary words.		
Exemplars: Samples of work that aligns with mastery of the grade-level standard.		
Classroom Library: The library is attractive, well-designed, and organized. The library has a variety of interesting books and short texts at different levels with new books displayed throughout the room. Books are easily accessible to students.		
Student Recognition: Teacher highlights student work and accomplishments of the students in the room.		
Student Supports: Create and use anchor charts, hint walls, and reminders in the room to guide students during independent practice.		
Celebrate Students: Teachers regularly recognize and celebrate students' growth and effort.		

Instruction: Do Now	Got It!	Possible Area of Focus
Do-Now: The Do-Now should only last 5-7 minutes.		
Knowledge: The Do-Now is time to activate or check prior knowledge, build background knowledge, and review vocabulary relevant to lesson.		
Pre-Assessment: Short, quick pre-assessments can be used to determine needs and gaps in students' learning.		

Instruction: Mini-Lesson	Got It!	Possible Area of Focus
Teacher Clarity: Teacher clearly states the learning target at the beginning of the lesson, states the rationale, and gives clear descriptions of what strong work looks like. Students must be able to answer 3 questions: 1) What am I learning today? 2) Why am I learning this? 3) How will I know if I learned it?		
Teacher Clarity: Teacher helps the students understand the learning targets by showing student work and examining exemplars, helping students apply clear descriptions of what strong work looks like, and providing feedback focused on the learning targets.		
Knowledge: Teacher activates or checks prior knowledge, builds background knowledge, and reviews vocabulary relevant to lesson. Note: this part of the lesson can take place as the Do-Now. Pre-assessment allows the teacher to determine what to teach, who to teach, and how to teach to promote learning.		
Explicit Teaching: Teacher thoroughly explains, demonstrates, and models the skill. The teacher connects new learning to previous learning targets, reviews information, previews and interacts with new knowledge, reviews foundational skills and vocabulary, and chunks content into small segments.		
Anchor Charts: Teacher creates anchor charts on chart paper or whiteboard in order to capture key points of the mini-lesson.		
Active Engagement: Teacher builds in many opportunities for all students to respond: whiteboards, choral responses, hand signals, numbered heads, turn and talk, and pair shares.		
Data- Driven: Teacher makes an immediate adjustment to the lesson based on student responses and evidence of learning.		
Engagement Practices: Teacher engages the students with evidence of teacher planning for engagement: pacing, teacher enthusiasm for the content, teacher passion for teaching, teacher energy, and/or student note-taking, pair shares, and discussion.		

Student Evidence (*students can*): Show evidence from Do-Now, explain the learning target and why it is important, discuss in pairs, take notes, formulate questions, initiate other students in the discussion, challenge each other's thinking, make contributions to the discussion, and justify and explain their answers.		
End of Mini-Lesson: Teacher reviews various supports for students in the room and clearly communicates expectations for practice. The teacher reviews transition procedures, the learning target, key teaching points, and the importance of the lesson.		

Instruction: Practice (small groups and independent learning)	Got It!	Possible Area of Focus
Smooth Transition: Transition from whole group to small group occurs smoothly with little to no loss of instructional time with the students assuming the responsibility.		
Time: Teacher maximizes instructional time with efficient classroom procedures and routines. Materials are prepared in advance and ready for the students.		
Learning Target: Teacher reinforces learning target throughout the lesson, links target to assignment or task, and uses the target to monitor learning. Feedback is aligned to the learning target.		
Engagement Practices: Teacher plans for engagement with small groups and independent work well-organized. There is evidence of clear, precise expectations for seat work (posted and reviewed), teacher circulating, and teacher reinforces effort and provides recognition. The teacher notices and reacts when the students are not engaged, increases students' opportunity to respond, maintains a lively pace, and keeps an eye on all students at all times.		
Learning Tasks or Assignments: The assignment or task is aligned to the grade level priority standards. The tasks involve thinking, problem-solving, reading, writing, and discussing.		
Instructional Resources & Materials: Teacher provides support for students during independent work: graphic organizers, sentence frames, notebooks, manipulatives, rubrics, computers, and anchor charts.		
Extending Thinking: Teacher provides activities and resources to extend student learning while providing students with resources and guidance.		
Collaboration: Students work in pairs or groups to engage in discussions and problem solving, use each other as academic resources, and communicate using academic language and vocabulary,		

Assessment for Learning: The teacher monitors all students, and regularly conferences or interviews with students to check on their learning and offer feedback.		
Questioning: Teacher asks high-quality questions that are prepared in advance, aligned to the learning targets, and cause all students to think and reflect. The teacher allows wait time (wait time 1) after asking a question and wait time (wait time 2) after the student answers the question.		
Student Evidence (*students can*): Students explain what they are doing, why, and what success looks like; work on challenging assignments aligned to the target; use scaffolds, answer text-dependent questions, and use evidence from text.		

Instruction: Closure with Evidence of Learning	Got It!	Possible Area of Focus
Sharing of Work: Students share their work with the teacher or their peers.		
Feedback: Teachers and peers provide specific, timely feedback to students that are aligned to the expectations of quality work.		
Self-Assessment: Students interpret scores with learning targets, track and monitor progress, self-reflect on process and effort, and set learning goals.		
Celebration: Teachers and students celebrate high-quality work and growth.		

Step 3: Reflect on, Discuss, and Create Action Plan

<table>
<tr><td>Read Teacher Framework, Take Notes, and Reflect on Practice</td></tr>
<tr><td></td></tr>
<tr><td>Teacher Select an Area of Focus To Improve Learning</td></tr>
<tr><td>Circle one

Environment   Do-Now   Mini-Lesson   Deliberate Practice   Closure with Evidence</td></tr>
<tr><td>Teacher Action Plan: Area of Focus, Success Criteria Indicator, and Plan</td></tr>
<tr><td></td></tr>
<tr><td>Evidence of Practice and Reflections</td></tr>
<tr><td></td></tr>
</table>

Step 4: Post the proficiency scales within the classroom, visit other rooms to see exemplary scales, and review Proficiency Scales guide.

This framework adapts ideas from Robert Marzano's research and Marzano Resources publications

Learning Block Plan -The Team Meeting to the Classroom	
Tasks to be Completed	**Check**
Teachers discuss and select priority standards for the upcoming learning block.	
Learning targets are formulated based on the deconstructed standards.	
Learning targets break down the priority standard into manageable segments of information.	
The teacher evaluates the cognitive demand associated with each learning target.	
The established learning target signifies mastery of the learning standard.	
The teacher creates approaching standard learning targets, which clearly articulate the prerequisite skills and vocabulary needed to master the standard. Teachers must teach the guaranteed vocabulary.	
The teacher creates a plan to push students' thinking beyond mastery of the standard.	

Proficiency Scales in the Classroom

Adult Actions	Check
The standards wall is organized, clearly articulated, consistently located, and accessible to students.	
Mastery is defined as the grade-level expectation.	
Mastery is the learning target created from the priority standard.	
Mastery of the standard is expressed through student friendly learning goals displayed on the standards wall	
Clear descriptions of what strong work looks like are available for students.	
Approaching the standard includes the prerequisite skills and vocabulary aligned with the mastery of the standard. Both must be taught.	
Beyond the Standard involves thinking that goes beyond the standard, articulated in student friendly learning goals	

Using the Proficiency Scales as an Instructional Tool	
Adult and Student Actions	**Check**
Teacher Action: The teacher reviews learning targets and clear descriptions of what strong work looks like at the start, during, and conclusion of the lesson.	
Teacher Action: Feedback from the teacher is aligned with the learning targets.	
Teacher Actions: Formative assessments are aligned with the learning targets.	
Student Action: Students can articulate the learning targets.	
Student Action: Students can explain how the task aligns to the learning targets.	
Student Action: Students use the descriptions of what strong work looks like to assess their learning.	
Student Action: Students set goals and track progress.	
Student Action: Students understand their current level of performance.	
Student Action: Students and staff celebrate their success and their growth.	

Step 5: Engage in instructional rounds by visiting other classrooms to enhance your instructional methods.

Instructional Rounds Agenda

Outcome: Observe classrooms, discuss, and reflect on practice.	Norms: • Maximize time. • Respect others. • Refrain from conversations with other observers. Refrain from interrupting the lesson. • Collect factual evidence. • Do not share evidence of observation outside the team.
Pre-Rounds Collaborative Meeting	Introduce the team. Read and discuss to build shared knowledge. Discuss the rounds documents. Review norms.
Rounds in the classroom	Adhere to the norms. Read, respond, and take notes.
Post-rounds collaborative meeting in the hallway	Discuss observed strengths. Reflect on instructional practice: Which parts of your teaching do you feel good about after visiting the classroom?

<table>
<tr><td></td><td>What new ideas do you have after visiting the classroom?</td></tr>
<tr><td colspan="2">Notes:</td></tr>
</table>

Bo Ryan

Collaborative Instructional Rounds Template

Grade-Level Team:	Date of Instructional Rounds:
Facilitator:	Time:

Norms for Instructional Rounds:

• Refrain from conversations with other observers.

• Refrain from interrupting the lesson.

• Collect factual evidence.

• Do not share evidence of observation outside the team.

Focus of the Instructional Round: Proficiency Scales and Instruction

Evidence Collected:

Strengths Observed (factual):	One or Two Positives for a Sticky Note:

Teacher Reflection Questions:

Which parts of my teaching do I feel good about after visiting the classroom?	What new ideas do I have after visiting the classroom?

Revised from The Brilliance in the Building © 2023 Solution Tree Press •

Phase 4: Data Action

Reflecting and Taking Action based on the Data

8 steps for having a successful meeting about taking Data Action

Step 1: Begin with greetings, conduct a check-in, and then set expectations and guidelines.

Step 2: Review the priority standards and the Common Formative Assessment (CFA).

Step 3: Analyze the data.

Step 4: Reflect on the findings from the data.

Step 5: Conduct a fidelity check to see if the team committed to the instructional plan.

Step 6: Create a plan for additional time and support.

Step 7: Organize a celebration for both students and staff.

Step 8: Taking data action is exemplary professional learning. In addition, arrange for professional development opportunities focused on data.

<u>Data Action</u>: Use the Data to Take Action

<u>Purpose:</u> In a healthy school culture, staff must know the current level of all students in order to make changes focused on student learning.

<u>Directions:</u> The data action process is for all certified teachers in the school at all grade levels: grade-level teams, subject-specific teams, singleton teachers, and humanities teachers. All staff must have a system to monitor student learning on a regular basis. Staff use the allotted time during the day to create, administer, and score common formative assessments. Teams then follow the steps in this tool to monitor student learning and to create a plan to support growth in all students.

Step 1: Greetings

Accountability Log		
Dates Met/Times	**Location Met**	**Staff Present**

Greeting/Check-In	Norms Review	Roles	Outcome

Step 2: Review Priority Standards and CFA

Priority Standards and Guaranteed Vocabulary taught during Learning Cycle
Describe Common Formative Assessment or Performance Assessment with Standard

Step 3: Review Data

Teacher's names	Number of Students who took the Assessment	Number of students at Mastery or Above	Number of students Not There Yet	Percentage of students at mastery or higher
Total:				
Data Story: Discuss student growth (pre, mid, post). Reflect on staff and student attendance.				

Step 4: Reflect on the Data

Data Reflection: What adjustments do we need to make in our practices to respond to these results for all students? Please include a reflection on the reliability and validity of common formative assessments, classroom instruction, and a plan for more time, support, and enrichment.
What is your strategic plan to address achievement disparities between our student groups, especially our poor and minority students?
What are the names of these students who are not at mastery?

Step 5: Fidelity Check: Reflect on your practices

Reflect on your Learning Plan and Conduct a Fidelity Check					
Did ALL students have access to Grade-Level Instruction?	Did you use the data to reflect on and make changes to your instruction?	Did staff follow the plan for more time and support?	Did staff administer a reliable and valid Pre-CFA?	Did staff administer a reliable and valid MID-CFA?	Did you meet with your team on a regular basis?
Yes No	Yes No	Yes No	Yes No	Yes No	Yes No

Step 6: Plan for More Time and Support

Plan for Flex Block			
Date of Flex Block	Whole Class Review of Assessment	Plan for Students who did **not** learn	Plan for Students who **did** learn

Plan for More Time and Support with Team			
Date of Team Meeting	Staff in Attendance	Plan for Students who need more time and support	Plan for students who need enrichment and extension

Step 7: Plan for Celebrations

Celebrations based on the Data		
Students Growth	Students Mastery	Teammate of the Cycle

Revised from Ryan, B (2023). **Brilliance in the building: Effecting change in urban schools using the PLC process. Solution tree.**

Phase 5: Next Steps for Continuous Learning

Continuous Learning Plan Aligned to our Learning Cycles

Purpose: Select professional learning that is job-embedded, research-based, reflective, goal of teaching others, individual, and subject-specific.

Directions: Staff, based on where they are currently in the cycle, select their own professional learning. Staff also select professional learning based on student data.

Planning: Ensure a Guaranteed and Viable Curriculum					
Continue to Work on Learning Plan		Collaborate on lesson plans.		Create Proficiency Scales	
Create a plan for more time and support.		Create exemplars, models, or worked examples of grade-level assignments.		Prepare small group instruction.	
Prepare sentence starters for writing and discussions.		Create Anchor Charts		Create Word Wall and Vocabulary Wall	
Study the curriculum		Create Scaffolds		Create a well-organized learning environment.	
Instruction: Ensuring High-Quality Instruction					
Set, review, and reflect on Instructional Goals with Teacher Framework.		Create Proficiency Scales in the Classroom and observe other proficiency scales in other classrooms.		Use Avanti - a tool for new staff.	

Video the lesson for you to observe and reflect on the instruction		Conduct Instructional Rounds		Ensure students have the tools to self-grade, chart progress, and celebrate success.	
Collaborate to create behavior-specific lessons.		Use AI to create student tasks that align with standards.		Work with a colleague to give feedback or to visit the classroom to share with you.	

Monitor Learning: Common Formative Assessment

Create Common Formative Assessments		Create Pre/Mid/End Common Formative Assessments.		Create Assessments aligned to proficiency scales.	
Review and reread the Common Formative Assessment Tool.		Collaboratively score not only CFAs but also writing assignments.		Share work samples with your team.	

Data Action: End-of-Block Data team

End of Learning Block Data Meeting		Create extension plans		Create Flex Block Plan	
College Prep Progress Monitoring.		Create plans for more time and support.		Reflect on other data sources.	

Reflection on time spent reading, writing, and discussing.		Quick Data Team Process.		Prepare for student retake.	

Continuous Learning for ALL: Support Staff

Create SPED Plans		Analyze Time		Call as many families as possible for positive reasons.	
Collaborate with others focused on learning.		Prep SPED PPT.		Work on SPED BIPS/FBAs/504s.	
Book Study with Action Focus.		Read educational magazines or books.		Utilize a PLC Resource Center.	

Teach Others: Become an Expert

Write a blog		Conduct Action Research:		Create a video documenting your success to share with others.	
Arrange room for Instructional Fairs.		Arrange the room for the instructional round visit.		Create a model classroom and invite visitors.	
Create a short podcast.		Share Student Learning Samples		Assist other teams and teachers with the process.	
Earn HRT: High Reliability Teaching Certificate and		Become an assessment expert and share with others.		Become an instructional Goal-Setting Expert.	

coaching others.				
Become a data expert and share the process with others.	Become an expert at writing IEPs and share with others.		Offer support to new teachers.	
Share your professional learning with others.	Become an expert on the state testing format and test-specific questions and share with others.		Become a subject-specific expert and share with others.	

Summary of your Learning for the Learning Cycle

Staff Meetings or Professional Learning Sessions Outside the School Day or ½ days	
Vertical Team Meetings (start and end of cycles)	
Professional Development Choice - collaborative or individual	
Teach Others	

Staff Celebrations	
Staff Created Professional Development	
Action Plan based on options above	

Learning Block 2

Dates	
SMART Goal	

Phase 1: Planning

Ensure a Guaranteed and Viable Curriculum

8 Action Steps for a successful learning plan meeting:

Step 1: Begin by greeting one another, conducting a check-in, revisiting established norms, and discussing desired outcomes.

Step 2: Examine the curriculum in detail.

Step 3: Engage in discussions to review and prioritize standards.

Step 4: Develop proficiency scales for sharing within the classroom.

Step 5: Outline the pacing for the unit.

Step 6: Formulate an instructional plan.

Step 7: Plan for additional time and support.

Step 8: Collaboratively planning a block of time is exemplary professional learning. In addition, organize your professional development to align with the planning.

Learning Plan

<u>Purpose:</u> Allow staff members to plan to create a guaranteed and viable curriculum, which ensures that all students have access to the curriculum and the time to learn it. Educational researcher and author Dr. Robert Marzano states that it is the number one factor impacting student learning.

<u>Directions:</u> The learning plan is for all certified teachers in the school in all grade levels: grade-level teams, subject-specific teams, singleton teachers, and humanities teachers. Staff use the allotted time during the day to study and take notes on the curriculum, review priority standards, create mastery models of expected student work, create a pacing guide, and create an instructional plan. This is also a tool that can be used by coaches to guide teachers and offer support. The teacher leads this process.

Step 1: Greetings

Accountability Log		
Dates Met/Times	**Location Met**	**Staff Present at Meeting**

Greeting/Check-In	Norms Review	Roles	Outcome

Step 2: Curriculum

Study the Curriculum Materials and Take Notes

Step 3: Discuss and Review Priority Standards

List Priority Standards for Cycle of Learning with GUARANTEED Vocabulary that must be taught (post in room)	
Priority Standards	Guaranteed Vocabulary
Learning Targets Created from the Standard(s)	

Process for Creating Proficiency Scales to ensure guaranteed and viable curriculum:

1) Write the learning target for mastery of standards
2) Write success criteria for mastery: what does good work look like with mastery models
3) Determine vocabulary, teach vocabulary simpler procedures, and prerequisite content
4) Discuss thinking beyond mastery with examples of exceeding
5) Discuss scaffolds for each target and teaching tips

Step 4: Create Learning Progression and Proficiency Scales

Learning Target	Approaching Standard Prerequisite Skills Guaranteed Vocabulary	Mastery of Standard w/Success Criteria	Exceeding Standard Thinking beyond mastery	Scaffolds for the Learning Targets & Teaching Tips for Exceeding Assignments
LT1				
Mastery Model, Exemplary, or Worked Example of Learning Target				
LT2				
Mastery Model, Exemplary, or Worked Example of Learning Target				
LT3				
Mastery Model, Exemplary, or Worked Example of Learning Target				
LT4				
Mastery Model, Exemplary, or Worked Example of Learning Target				

Step 5: Create Pacing for the Block

- **Examine** the curriculum, district assessment calendar, and overall district calendar.

- **Outline the schedule** for teaching learning targets, conducting common formative assessments, and allocating time for data monitoring and reflection.

- **Designate specific days** for teaching particular standards and strategize on how to assess learning through common formative assessments.

- **Identify anticipated team meeting days** and ensure alignment of professional development with these plans: review and develop the learning cycle plan, create and implement common formative assessments, analyze and reflect on the data, and formulate a data-driven action plan.

- **This collaborative strategy must be mutually agreed upon** and adhered to by the team. If they cannot, they follow the curriculum as closely as possible or ask an instructional coach for additional support and expertise.

Focus:		Number of Days:		
Pacing of Cycle from _________ to _________				
Monday	Tuesday	Wednesday	Thursday	Friday

Step 6: Create an Instructional Plan

<table>
<tr><td colspan="2" align="center">Instructional Plan</td></tr>
<tr><td>

- How will you ensure <u>ALL</u> students have access to grade-level assignments?

- How will your team enrich and extend the learning of students beyond mastery?

- What teaching practices work best for this specific priority standard?

- Plan small-group instruction and/or conferences for students not at mastery.

Small Group Math   Small Group Literacy

</td></tr>
<tr><td>

</td></tr>
</table>

Step 7: Create a Plan for More Time and Support:

Systematic Plan for More Time and Support		
Focus	Teaching Plan	Monitor Progress
More Time and Support on grade-level priority standards		
More time and Support on Prerequisite Skills are needed to master grade-level standards		
Fluency Repeated Reading Program		
Enrichment		
IEP Plans		
Arts		
Action Plan		

Revised from Ryan, B (2023). Brilliance in the building: Effecting change in urban schools using the PLC process. Solution tree.

Phase 2: Measuring Learning

Creating, Administering, and Scoring Common Formative Assessments

6 steps for having a successful meeting about common formative assessments:

Step 1: Begin by greeting one another, conducting a check-in, revisiting established norms, and discussing desired outcomes.

Step 2: Examine the criteria for developing common formative assessments (CFAs)

Step 3: Develop a CFA(s).

Step 4: Consider the reliability and validity of the CFA.

Step 5: Review, reflect, and agree on shared commitments.

Step 6: Creating common formative assessments is considered exemplary professional learning. In addition, organize a professional learning plan aligned to assessments.

Measuring Learning with Common Formative Assessments

Purpose: The purpose of the grade-level common formative assessment is to measure student learning of the guaranteed and viable curriculum. This tool gives all stakeholders shared knowledge of how to create a reliable and valid common formative assessment. The entire staff can use this in order to create common formative assessments.

Directions: Review the criteria below to support your creation of common formative assessments or performance assessments.

Step 1: Greetings

Accountability Log		
Dates Met/Times	**Location Met**	**Staff Present**

Greeting/Check-In	Norms Review	Roles	Outcome

Step 2: Examine the criteria for developing common formative assessments (CFAs)

Check	Success Criteria for an Exemplary Common Formative Assessment
	The team/teacher discusses and identifies priority standard (s) to be measured.
	The team/teacher writes the assessment around a priority standard.
	The team/teacher evaluates the depth of knowledge level (DOK) of the target(s), selects the best strategy for assessing the target (selected response, constructed response, a combination, or performance task), and aligns the assessment to the rigor of the standard.
	The team/teacher creates the assessment items that match the level of thinking of the target (determine DOK level and align to the level of demand of the question).
	The team/teacher agrees on what mastery will look like for the priority standards and the overall assessment with clear success criteria.
	The team/teacher identifies the academic language and vocabulary that need to be targeted.
	The team ensures the CFA meets the criteria: 1- 2 constructed responses, 2-4 selected responses, or a combination of both per assessment.
	The team/teacher creates an assessment that is neat, organized, and easy to read with adequate space to write and solve problems. The directions and questions are clearly written. The learning target(s) are written on the assessment.
	The team/teacher creates an assessment that is quick to administer, appropriate for the time allotted, and easy to score.
	The students must be a part of the assessment process: clarity on mastery of the standard, review of the assessment, opportunity to retake, and time in the schedule for flex time for reteaching from the teacher. Students set goals and celebrate growth.

Success Criteria for an Exemplary Performance Assessment	
	The team/teacher determines the focus of the performance assessment.
	The team/teacher makes sure the assessment aligns with the priority standard.
	The team/teacher is clear about what the students must demonstrate for mastery.
	The team/teacher creates success criteria to describe the expectations of mastery.
	The team/teacher assesses the students by observation or examining a product.
	The team/teacher will share examples of the performance assessment.

Revised from Ryan, B (2023). Brilliance in the building: Effecting change in urban schools using the PLC process. Solution tree.

Step 3: Develop a CFA.

<u>Common Formative Assessment Framework Model</u>

Student Name:		Date:	Grade:

Name of CFA:

<u>Standard:</u>

<u>Precise Directions for CFA:</u>

<u>Questions Aligned to LT</u>

Review the Learning Plan and Share Links of your Common Formative Assessments for this Cycle			
Pre-CFA	Mid-CFA	Additional CFA	End-CFA

Step 4: Review Common Formative Assessments and Formative Assessments for Reliability and Validity

The essence of assessments lies in ensuring they are both reliable and valid.

- **<u>Validity:</u>** This refers to the extent to which an assessment accurately measures what the team believes students should have learned, ensuring alignment with instructional goals.

- **<u>Reliability:</u>** This indicates that students who demonstrate understanding of the concepts have genuinely grasped them.

Three Intentional Steps for Developing Valid and Reliable Assessments:

- Identify the learning target.

- Determine the level of rigor of the target.

- Decide on the types and quantity of items for the assessment.

Evaluating the Quality of an Assessment

Is it VALID?

We have pinpointed specific learning targets.

We have established the rigor level for each target.

The assessment items correspond to the cognitive demands of the learning targets.

Is it RELIABLE?

We utilized a sufficient number of questions to ensure reliability.

The team has reached a consensus on the criteria for mastery.

The reading levels of the questions do not hinder the assessment.

Adapted from the work of Ainsworth, Bailey, Erkens, Ferriter, Jakicic, Kramer, Schuhl, Kanold, Barnes, Toncheff, Marzano, Buffum, Malone, Strong, Vagle, Marzano CEU Course on Formative Assessments, Global PD videos, Stronge and Associates, and Global PD Mini-Course on CFA

Step 5: Review, reflect, and agree on shared commitments.

Common Formative Assessment Team Commitments	
Yes, I commit	**Team Member Commitments**
	We agree that the common formative assessment measures grade-level learning for all students.
	We agree that the common formative assessment meets the success criteria listed on page —
	We agree that the common formative assessment created is both reliable and viable.
	We agree to implement the assessment on the same date and time. Date of CFA: Times:
	We agree to give the same directions to our students before the CFA.
	We agree to allow the following amount of time for the assessment:
	We agree to supply the following materials for the students:
	We agree that all students will take the CFA in the classroom.
	We agree on the following scoring plan for the CFA________________ with mastery level ________________.

<table>
<tr><td></td><td>We agree to collaboratively score the assessment with our team on the following dates _____________________ in the following location_______________.</td></tr>
<tr><td></td><td>We agree or disagree to allow students to self-grade their assessments.</td></tr>
<tr><td></td><td>We agree that all students have the opportunity to retake the assessment.</td></tr>
<tr><td></td><td>We agree to the following timeline of the common formative assessments:

- Assessment Development:

- Administration of the CFA Window:

- Date to Collaboratively Score:

- Scoring Completion:

- Data Action Meeting:

- Flex Time on the following day:

- Instructional Adjustments Implemented:</td></tr>
</table>

Phase 3: Classroom Instruction

Ensuring High Quality Instruction in all Classrooms

6 Action Steps for a successful meeting focused on instruction:

Step 1: Begin by greeting one another, conducting a check-in, revisiting established norms, and discussing desired outcomes.

Step 2: Read, reflect, and review the Teacher Framework multiple times.

Step 3: Reflect on and discuss areas for improvement in your teaching practices using the Teacher Framework Success Criteria.

Step 4: Create and display the proficiency scales in your classroom, observe exemplary scales in other classrooms, and consult the Proficiency Scales guide.

Step 5: Engage in instructional rounds by visiting other classrooms to enhance your instructional methods.

Step 6: Ensuring high-quality instruction on a daily basis by creating instructional action plans and using proficiency scales is quality professional learning. In addition, organize your professional development to align with improving instruction.

Ensuring Effective Instruction in Every Classroom

<u>Purpose:</u> This section is designed for staff to meet as teams or individually to reflect on and improve classroom instruction. The goal is for every staff member to embrace continuous growth as a relentless learner and effective teacher.

<u>Directions:</u> Teachers read and reread the framework, then take notes in *the Reflection on Teaching section*. Teachers consider their current level of instruction, identify an area for growth, and create an action plan to improve your practice.

This phase draws heavily on the work of Robert Marzano's New Art and Science of Teaching and the PLC Framework from Solution Tree - Bo Ryan

Step 1: Greetings

Accountability Log		
Dates Met/Times	**Location Met**	**Staff Present at Meeting**

Greeting/Check-In	Norms Review	Roles	Outcome

Step 2: Read, reflect, and review the Teacher Framework multiple times.

Classroom Learning Environment	Got It!	Possible Area of Focus
Classroom Arrangement: The classroom is neat, safe, and well-organized.		
Standard Wall: The standards wall has the learning targets posted for the month written as student friendly learning goals with clear expectations for grade-level work.		
Do-Now: A brief activity is posted on standard wall or power point.		
Behavior Expectations: Behavior expectations are posted in the room.		
Word Walls: The wall shares high frequency words, words commonly misspelled in students' work, and academic vocabulary words.		
Exemplars: Samples of work that aligns with mastery of the grade-level standard.		
Classroom Library: The library is attractive, well-designed, and organized. The library has a variety of interesting books and short texts at different levels with new books displayed throughout the room. Books are easily accessible to students.		
Student Recognition: Teacher highlights student work and accomplishments of the students in the room.		
Student Supports: Create and use anchor charts, hint walls, and reminders in the room to guide students during independent practice.		
Celebrate Students: Teachers regularly recognize and celebrate students' growth and effort.		

Instruction: Do Now	Got It!	Possible Area of Focus
Do-Now: The Do-Now should only last 5-7 minutes.		
Knowledge: The Do-Now is time to activate or check prior knowledge, build background knowledge, and review vocabulary relevant to lesson.		
Pre-Assessment: Short, quick pre-assessments can be used to determine needs and gaps in students' learning.		

Instruction: Mini-Lesson	Got It!	Possible Area of Focus

Teacher Clarity: Teacher clearly states the learning target at the beginning of the lesson, states the rationale, and gives clear descriptions of what strong work looks like. Students must be able to answer 3 questions:
  1) What am I learning today?
  2) Why am I learning this?
  3) How will I know if I learned it?		

Teacher Clarity: Teacher helps the students understand the learning targets by showing student work and examining exemplars, helping students apply clear descriptions of what strong work looks like, and providing feedback focused on the learning targets.		
Knowledge: Teacher activates or checks prior knowledge, builds background knowledge, and reviews vocabulary relevant to lesson. Note: this part of the lesson can take place as the Do-Now. Pre-assessment allows the teacher to determine what to teach, who to teach, and how to teach to promote learning.		
Explicit Teaching: Teacher thoroughly explains, demonstrates, and models the skill. The teacher connects new learning to previous learning targets, reviews information, previews and interacts with new knowledge, reviews foundational skills and vocabulary, and chunks content into small segments.		
Anchor Charts: Teacher creates anchor charts on chart paper or whiteboard in order to capture key points of the mini-lesson.		
Active Engagement: Teacher builds in many opportunities for all students to respond: whiteboards, choral responses, hand signals, numbered heads, turn and talk, and pair shares.		
Data- Driven: Teacher makes an immediate adjustment to the lesson based on student responses and evidence of learning.		
Engagement Practices: Teacher engages the students with evidence of teacher planning for engagement: pacing, teacher enthusiasm for the content, teacher passion for teaching, teacher energy, and/or student note-taking, pair shares, and discussion.		

Student Evidence (*students can*): Show evidence from Do-Now, explain the learning target and why it is important, discuss in pairs, take notes, formulate questions, initiate other students in the discussion, challenge each other's thinking, make contributions to the discussion, and justify and explain their answers.		
End of Mini-Lesson: Teacher reviews various supports for students in the room and clearly communicates expectations for practice. The teacher reviews transition procedures, the learning target, key teaching points, and the importance of the lesson.		

Instruction: Practice (small groups and independent learning)	Got It!	Possible Area of Focus
Smooth Transition: Transition from whole group to small group occurs smoothly with little to no loss of instructional time with the students assuming the responsibility.		
Time: Teacher maximizes instructional time with efficient classroom procedures and routines. Materials are prepared in advance and ready for the students.		
Learning Target: Teacher reinforces learning target throughout the lesson, links target to assignment or task, and uses the target to monitor learning. Feedback is aligned to the learning target.		
Engagement Practices: Teacher plans for engagement with small groups and independent work well-organized. There is evidence of clear, precise expectations for seat work (posted and reviewed), teacher circulating, and teacher reinforces effort and provides recognition. The teacher notices and reacts when the students are not engaged, increases students' opportunity to respond, maintains a lively pace, and keeps an eye on all students at all times.		
Learning Tasks or Assignments: The assignment or task is aligned to the grade level priority standards. The tasks involve thinking, problem-solving, reading, writing, and discussing.		
Instructional Resources & Materials: Teacher provides support for students during independent work: graphic organizers, sentence frames, notebooks, manipulatives, rubrics, computers, and anchor charts.		
Extending Thinking: Teacher provides activities and resources to extend student learning while providing students with resources and guidance.		
Collaboration: Students work in pairs or groups to engage in discussions and problem solving, use each other as academic resources, and communicate using academic language and vocabulary,		

Assessment for Learning: The teacher monitors all students, and regularly conferences or interviews with students to check on their learning and offer feedback.		
Questioning: Teacher asks high-quality questions that are prepared in advance, aligned to the learning targets, and cause all students to think and reflect. The teacher allows wait time (wait time 1) after asking a question and wait time (wait time 2) after the student answers the question.		
Student Evidence (*students can*): Students explain what they are doing, why, and what success looks like; work on challenging assignments aligned to the target; use scaffolds, answer text-dependent questions, and use evidence from text.		

Instruction: Closure with Evidence of Learning	Got It!	Possible Area of Focus
Sharing of Work: Students share their work with the teacher or their peers.		
Feedback: Teachers and peers provide specific, timely feedback to students that are aligned to the expectations of quality work.		
Self-Assessment: Students interpret scores with learning targets, track and monitor progress, self-reflect on process and effort, and set learning goals.		
Celebration: Teachers and students celebrate high-quality work and growth.		

Step 3: Reflect on, Discuss, and Create Action Plan

<table>
<tr><td>

Read Teacher Framework, Take Notes, and Reflect on Practice

</td></tr>
<tr><td>

</td></tr>
<tr><td>

Teacher Select an Area of Focus To Improve Learning

</td></tr>
<tr><td>

Circle one

Environment   **Do-Now**   **Mini-Lesson**   **Deliberate Practice**   **Closure with Evidence**

</td></tr>
<tr><td>

Teacher Action Plan: Area of Focus, Success Criteria Indicator, and Plan

</td></tr>
<tr><td>

</td></tr>
<tr><td>

Evidence of Practice and Reflections

</td></tr>
<tr><td>

</td></tr>
</table>

Step 4: Post the proficiency scales within the classroom, visit other rooms to see exemplary scales, and review Proficiency Scales guide.

This framework adapts ideas from Robert Marzano's research and Marzano Resources publications

Learning Block Plan -The Team Meeting to the Classroom

Tasks to be Completed	Check
Teachers discuss and select priority standards for the upcoming learning block.	
Learning targets are formulated based on the deconstructed standards.	
Learning targets break down the priority standard into manageable segments of information.	
The teacher evaluates the cognitive demand associated with each learning target.	
The established learning target signifies mastery of the learning standard.	
The teacher creates approaching standard learning targets, which clearly articulate the prerequisite skills and vocabulary needed to master the standard. Teachers must teach the guaranteed vocabulary.	
The teacher creates a plan to push students' thinking beyond mastery of the standard.	

Proficiency Scales in the Classroom

Adult Actions	Check
The standards wall is organized, clearly articulated, consistently located, and accessible to students.	
Mastery is defined as the grade-level expectation.	
Mastery is the learning target created from the priority standard.	
Mastery of the standard is expressed through student friendly learning goals displayed on the standards wall	
Clear descriptions of what strong work looks like are available for students.	
Approaching the standard includes the prerequisite skills and vocabulary aligned with the mastery of the standard. Both must be taught.	
Beyond the Standard involves thinking that goes beyond the standard, articulated in student friendly learning goals	

<table>
<tr><th colspan="2">Using the Proficiency Scales as an Instructional Tool</th></tr>
<tr><th>Adult and Student Actions</th><th>Check</th></tr>
<tr><td>Teacher Action: The teacher reviews learning targets and clear descriptions of what strong work looks like at the start, during, and conclusion of the lesson.</td><td></td></tr>
<tr><td>Teacher Action: Feedback from the teacher is aligned with the learning targets.</td><td></td></tr>
<tr><td>Teacher Actions: Formative assessments are aligned with the learning targets.</td><td></td></tr>
<tr><td>Student Action: Students can articulate the learning targets.</td><td></td></tr>
<tr><td>Student Action: Students can explain how the task aligns to the learning targets.</td><td></td></tr>
<tr><td>Student Action: Students use the descriptions of what strong work looks like to assess their learning.</td><td></td></tr>
<tr><td>Student Action: Students set goals and track progress.</td><td></td></tr>
<tr><td>Student Action: Students understand their current level of performance.</td><td></td></tr>
<tr><td>Student Action: Students and staff celebrate their success and their growth.</td><td></td></tr>
</table>

Step 5: Engage in instructional rounds by visiting other classrooms to enhance your instructional methods.

Instructional Rounds Agenda

Outcome: Observe classrooms, discuss, and reflect on practice.	Norms: • Maximize time. • Respect others. • Refrain from conversations with other observers. Refrain from interrupting the lesson. • Collect factual evidence. • Do not share evidence of observation outside the team.
Pre-Rounds Collaborative Meeting	Introduce the team. Read and discuss to build shared knowledge. Discuss the rounds documents. Review norms.
Rounds in the classroom	Adhere to the norms. Read, respond, and take notes.
Post-rounds collaborative meeting in the hallway	Discuss observed strengths. Reflect on instructional practice: Which parts of your teaching do you feel good about after visiting the classroom?

	What new ideas do you have after visiting the classroom?
Notes:	

Bo Ryan

Collaborative Instructional Rounds Template

Grade-Level Team:	Date of Instructional Rounds:
Facilitator:	Time:

Norms for Instructional Rounds:

• Refrain from conversations with other observers.

• Refrain from interrupting the lesson.

• Collect factual evidence.

• Do not share evidence of observation outside the team.

Focus of the Instructional Round: Proficiency Scales and Instruction

Evidence Collected:

Strengths Observed (factual):	One or Two Positives for a Sticky Note:

Teacher Reflection Questions:

Which parts of my teaching do I feel good about after visiting the classroom?	What new ideas do I have after visiting the classroom?

Phase 4: Data Action

Reflecting and Taking Action based on the Data

8 steps for having a successful meeting about taking Data Action

Step 1: Begin with greetings, conduct a check-in, and then set expectations and guidelines.

Step 2: Review the priority standards and the Common Formative Assessment (CFA).

Step 3: Analyze the data.

Step 4: Reflect on the findings from the data.

Step 5: Conduct a fidelity check to see if the team committed to the instructional plan.

Step 6: Create a plan for additional time and support.

Step 7: Organize a celebration for both students and staff.

Step 8: Taking data action is exemplary professional learning. In addition, arrange for professional development opportunities focused on data.

<u>Data Action</u>: Use the Data to Take Action

<u>Purpose</u>: In a healthy school culture, staff must know the current level of all students in order to make changes focused on student learning.

<u>Directions</u>: The data action process is for all certified teachers in the school at all grade levels: grade-level teams, subject-specific teams, singleton teachers, and humanities teachers. All staff must have a system to monitor student learning on a regular basis. Staff use the allotted time during the day to create, administer, and score common formative assessments. Teams then follow the steps in this tool to monitor student learning and to create a plan to support growth in all students.

Step 1: Greetings

Accountability Log		
Dates Met/Times	**Location Met**	**Staff Present**

Greeting/Check-In	Norms Review	Roles	Outcome

Step 2: Review Priority Standards and CFA

Priority Standards and Guaranteed Vocabulary taught during Learning Cycle
Describe Common Formative Assessment or Performance Assessment with Standard

Step 3: Review Data

Teacher's names	Number of Students who took the Assessment	Number of students at Mastery or Above	Number of students Not There Yet	Percentage of students at mastery or higher
Total:				
Data Story: Discuss student growth (pre, mid, post). Reflect on staff and student attendance.				

Step 4: Reflect on the Data

Data Reflection: What adjustments do we need to make in our practices to respond to these results for all students? Please include a reflection on the reliability and validity of common formative assessments, classroom instruction, and a plan for more time, support, and enrichment.
What is your strategic plan to address achievement disparities between our student groups, especially our poor and minority students?
What are the names of these students who are not at mastery?

Step 5: Fidelity Check: Reflect on your practices

Reflect on your Learning Plan and Conduct a Fidelity Check					
Did ALL students have access to Grade-Level Instruction?	Did you use the data to reflect on and make changes to your instruction?	Did staff follow the plan for more time and support?	Did staff administer a reliable and valid Pre-CFA?	Did staff administer a reliable and valid MID-CFA?	Did you meet with your team on a regular basis?
Yes No	Yes No	Yes No	Yes No	Yes No	Yes No

Step 6: Plan for More Time and Support

Plan for Flex Block			
Date of Flex Block	Whole Class Review of Assessment	Plan for Students who did **not** learn	Plan for Students who **did** learn

Plan for More Time and Support with Team			
Date of Team Meeting	Staff in Attendance	Plan for Students who need more time and support	Plan for students who need enrichment and extension

Step 7: Plan for Celebrations

Celebrations based on the Data		
Students Growth	Students Mastery	Teammate of the Cycle

Revised from Ryan, B (2023). **Brilliance in the building: Effecting change in urban schools using the PLC process. Solution tree.**

Phase 5: Next Steps for Continuous Learning

Continuous Learning Plan Aligned to our Learning Cycles

Purpose: Select professional learning that is job-embedded, research-based, reflective, goal of teaching others, individual, and subject-specific.

Directions: Staff, based on where they are currently in the cycle, select their own professional learning. Staff also select professional learning based on student data.

Planning: Ensure a Guaranteed and Viable Curriculum					
Continue to Work on Learning Plan		Collaborate on lesson plans.		Create Proficiency Scales	
Create a plan for more time and support.		Create exemplars, models, or worked examples of grade-level assignments.		Prepare small group instruction.	
Prepare sentence starters for writing and discussions.		Create Anchor Charts		Create Word Wall and Vocabulary Wall	
Study the curriculum		Create Scaffolds		Create a well-organized learning environment.	
Instruction: Ensuring High-Quality Instruction					
Set, review, and reflect on Instructional Goals with Teacher Framework.		Create Proficiency Scales in the Classroom and observe other proficiency scales in other classrooms.		Use Avanti - a tool for new staff.	

Video the lesson for you to observe and reflect on the instruction		Conduct Instructional Rounds		Ensure students have the tools to self-grade, chart progress, and celebrate success.
Collaborate to create behavior-specific lessons.		Use AI to create student tasks that align with standards.		Work with a colleague to give feedback or to visit the classroom to share with you.

Monitor Learning: Common Formative Assessment

Create Common Formative Assessments		Create Pre/Mid/End Common Formative Assessments.		Create Assessments aligned to proficiency scales.
Review and reread the Common Formative Assessment Tool.		Collaboratively score not only CFAs but also writing assignments.		Share work samples with your team.

Data Action: End-of-Block Data team

End of Learning Block Data Meeting		Create extension plans		Create Flex Block Plan
College Prep Progress Monitoring.		Create plans for more time and support.		Reflect on other data sources.
Reflection on time spent reading,		Quick Data Team		Prepare for student retake.

writing, and discussing.		Process.		

Continuous Learning for ALL: Support Staff	

Create SPED Plans		Analyze Time		Call as many families as possible for positive reasons.	
Collaborate with others focused on learning.		Prep SPED PPT.		Work on SPED BIPS/FBAs/504s.	
Book Study with Action Focus.		Read educational magazines or books.		Utilize a PLC Resource Center.	

Teach Others: Become an Expert	

Write a blog		Conduct Action Research:		Create a video documenting your success to share with others.	
Arrange room for Instructional Fairs.		Arrange the room for the instructional round visit.		Create a model classroom and invite visitors.	
Create a short podcast.		Share Student Learning Samples		Assist other teams and teachers with the process.	
Earn HRT: High Reliability Teaching Certificate and coaching others.		Become an assessment expert and share with others.		Become an instructional Goal-Setting Expert.	

Become a data expert and share the process with others.		Become an expert at writing IEPs and share with others.		Offer support to new teachers.	
Share your professional learning with others.		Become an expert on the state testing format and test-specific questions and share with others.		Become a subject-specific expert and share with others.	

Summary of your Learning for the Learning Cycle	
Staff Meetings or Professional Learning Sessions Outside the School Day or ½ days	
Vertical Team Meetings (start and end of cycles)	
Professional Development Choice - collaborative or individual	
Teach Others	
Staff Celebrations	

Staff Created Professional Development	
Action Plan based on options above	

Learning Block 3

Dates	
SMART Goal	

Phase 1: Planning

Ensure a Guaranteed and Viable Curriculum

8 Action Steps for a successful learning plan meeting:

Step 1: Begin by greeting one another, conducting a check-in, revisiting established norms, and discussing desired outcomes.

Step 2: Examine the curriculum in detail.

Step 3: Engage in discussions to review and prioritize standards.

Step 4: Develop proficiency scales for sharing within the classroom.

Step 5: Outline the pacing for the unit.

Step 6: Formulate an instructional plan.

Step 7: Plan for additional time and support.

Step 8: Collaboratively planning a block of time is exemplary professional learning. In addition, organize your professional development to align with the planning.

Learning Plan

Purpose: Allow staff members to plan to create a guaranteed and viable curriculum, which ensures that all students have access to the curriculum and the time to learn it. Educational researcher and author Dr. Robert Marzano states that it is the number one factor impacting student learning.

Directions: The learning plan is for all certified teachers in the school in all grade levels: grade-level teams, subject-specific teams, singleton teachers, and humanities teachers. Staff use the allotted time during the day to study and take notes on the curriculum, review priority standards, create mastery models of expected student work, create a pacing guide, and create an instructional plan. This is also a tool that can be used by coaches to guide teachers and offer support. The teacher leads this process.

Step 1: Greetings

Accountability Log		
Dates Met/Times	**Location Met**	**Staff Present at Meeting**

Greeting/Check-In	Norms Review	Roles	Outcome

Step 2: Curriculum

Study the Curriculum Materials and Take Notes

Step 3: Discuss and Review Priority Standards

<table>
<tr><td colspan="2" align="center">List Priority Standards for Cycle of Learning with GUARANTEED Vocabulary that must be taught
(post in room)</td></tr>
<tr><td>Priority Standards</td><td>Guaranteed Vocabulary</td></tr>
<tr><td></td><td></td></tr>
<tr><td colspan="2" align="center">Learning Targets Created from the Standard(s)

</td></tr>
</table>

Process for Creating Proficiency Scales to ensure guaranteed and viable curriculum:

1) Write the learning target for mastery of standards
2) Write success criteria for mastery: what does good work look like with mastery models
3) Determine vocabulary, teach vocabulary simpler procedures, and prerequisite content
4) Discuss thinking beyond mastery with examples of exceeding
5) Discuss scaffolds for each target and teaching tips

Step 4: Create Learning Progression and Proficiency Scales

Learning Target	Approaching Standard Prerequisite Skills Guaranteed Vocabulary	Mastery of Standard w/Success Criteria	Exceeding Standard Thinking beyond mastery	Scaffolds for the Learning Targets & Teaching Tips for Exceeding Assignments
LT1				
Mastery Model, Exemplary, or Worked Example of Learning Target				
LT2				
Mastery Model, Exemplary, or Worked Example of Learning Target				
LT3				
Mastery Model, Exemplary, or Worked Example of Learning Target				
LT4				
Mastery Model, Exemplary, or Worked Example of Learning Target				

Step 5: Create Pacing for the Block

- **Examine** the curriculum, district assessment calendar, and overall district calendar.

- **Outline the schedule** for teaching learning targets, conducting common formative assessments, and allocating time for data monitoring and reflection.

- **Designate specific days** for teaching particular standards and strategize on how to assess learning through common formative assessments.

- **Identify anticipated team meeting days** and ensure alignment of professional development with these plans: review and develop the learning cycle plan, create and implement common formative assessments, analyze and reflect on the data, and formulate a data-driven action plan.

- **This collaborative strategy must be mutually agreed upon** and adhered to by the team. If they cannot, they follow the curriculum as closely as possible or ask an instructional coach for additional support and expertise.

Focus:		Number of Days:		
Pacing of Cycle from _________ to _________				
Monday	Tuesday	Wednesday	Thursday	Friday

Step 6: Create an Instructional Plan

<table>
<tr><td colspan="1" align="center">Instructional Plan</td></tr>
<tr><td>

- How will you ensure <u>ALL</u> students have access to grade-level assignments?

- How will your team enrich and extend the learning of students beyond mastery?

- What teaching practices work best for this specific priority standard?

- Plan small-group instruction and/or conferences for students not at mastery.

Small Group Math   Small Group Literacy

</td></tr>
<tr><td>

</td></tr>
</table>

Step 7: Create a Plan for More Time and Support:

<table>
<tr><td colspan="3" align="center">Systematic Plan for More Time and Support</td></tr>
<tr><td align="center">Focus</td><td align="center">Teaching Plan</td><td align="center">Monitor Progress</td></tr>
<tr><td>More Time and Support on grade-level priority standards</td><td></td><td></td></tr>
<tr><td>More time and Support on Prerequisite Skills are needed to master grade-level standards</td><td></td><td></td></tr>
<tr><td>Fluency Repeated Reading Program</td><td></td><td></td></tr>
<tr><td>Enrichment</td><td></td><td></td></tr>
<tr><td>IEP Plans</td><td></td><td></td></tr>
<tr><td>Arts</td><td></td><td></td></tr>
<tr><td colspan="3" align="center">Action Plan</td></tr>
<tr><td colspan="3"></td></tr>
</table>

Revised from Ryan, B (2023). Brilliance in the building: Effecting change in urban schools using the PLC process. Solution tree.

Phase 2: Measuring Learning

Creating, Administering, and Scoring Common Formative Assessments

6 steps for having a successful meeting about common formative assessments:

Step 1: Begin by greeting one another, conducting a check-in, revisiting established norms, and discussing desired outcomes.

Step 2: Examine the criteria for developing common formative assessments (CFAs)

Step 3: Develop a CFA(s).

Step 4: Consider the reliability and validity of the CFA.

Step 5: Review, reflect, and agree on shared commitments.

Step 6: Creating common formative assessments is considered exemplary professional learning. In addition, organize a professional learning plan aligned to assessments.

Measuring Learning with Common Formative Assessments

Purpose: The purpose of the grade-level common formative assessment is to measure student learning of the guaranteed and viable curriculum. This tool gives all stakeholders shared knowledge of how to create a reliable and valid common formative assessment. The entire staff can use this in order to create common formative assessments.

Directions: Review the criteria below to support your creation of common formative assessments or performance assessments.

Step 1: Greetings

Accountability Log		
Dates Met/Times	**Location Met**	**Staff Present**

Greeting/Check-In	Norms Review	Roles	Outcome

Step 2: Examine the criteria for developing common formative assessments (CFAs)

Check	Success Criteria for an Exemplary Common Formative Assessment
	The team/teacher discusses and identifies priority standard (s) to be measured.
	The team/teacher writes the assessment around a priority standard.
	The team/teacher evaluates the depth of knowledge level (DOK) of the target(s), selects the best strategy for assessing the target (selected response, constructed response, a combination, or performance task), and aligns the assessment to the rigor of the standard.
	The team/teacher creates the assessment items that match the level of thinking of the target (determine DOK level and align to the level of demand of the question).
	The team/teacher agrees on what mastery will look like for the priority standards and the overall assessment with clear success criteria.
	The team/teacher identifies the academic language and vocabulary that need to be targeted.
	The team ensures the CFA meets the criteria: 1- 2 constructed responses, 2-4 selected responses, or a combination of both per assessment.
	The team/teacher creates an assessment that is neat, organized, and easy to read with adequate space to write and solve problems. The directions and questions are clearly written. The learning target(s) are written on the assessment.
	The team/teacher creates an assessment that is quick to administer, appropriate for the time allotted, and easy to score.
	The students must be a part of the assessment process: clarity on mastery of the standard, review of the assessment, opportunity to retake, and time in the schedule for flex time for reteaching from the teacher. Students set goals and celebrate growth.

Success Criteria for an Exemplary Performance Assessment	
	The team/teacher determines the focus of the performance assessment.

	The team/teacher makes sure the assessment aligns with the priority standard.
	The team/teacher is clear about what the students must demonstrate for mastery.
	The team/teacher creates success criteria to describe the expectations of mastery.
	The team/teacher assesses the students by observation or examining a product.
	The team/teacher will share examples of the performance assessment.

Revised from Ryan, B (2023). *Brilliance in the building: Effecting change in urban schools using the PLC process.* Solution tree.

Step 3: Develop a CFA.

<u>Common Formative Assessment Framework Model</u>

Student Name:	Date:	Grade:

Name of CFA:

<u>Standard:</u>

<u>Precise Directions for CFA:</u>

<u>Questions Aligned to LT</u>

Review the Learning Plan and Share Links of your Common Formative Assessments for this Cycle			
Pre-CFA	Mid-CFA	Additional CFA	End-CFA

Step 4: Review Common Formative Assessments and Formative Assessments for Reliability and Validity

The essence of assessments lies in ensuring they are both reliable and valid.

- **Validity:** This refers to the extent to which an assessment accurately measures what the team believes students should have learned, ensuring alignment with instructional goals.

- **Reliability:** This indicates that students who demonstrate understanding of the concepts have genuinely grasped them.

Three Intentional Steps for Developing Valid and Reliable Assessments:

- Identify the learning target.

- Determine the level of rigor of the target.

- Decide on the types and quantity of items for the assessment.

Evaluating the Quality of an Assessment

Is it VALID?

We have pinpointed specific learning targets.

We have established the rigor level for each target.

The assessment items correspond to the cognitive demands of the learning targets.

Is it RELIABLE?

We utilized a sufficient number of questions to ensure reliability.

The team has reached a consensus on the criteria for mastery.

The reading levels of the questions do not hinder the assessment.

Adapted from the work of Ainsworth, Bailey, Erkens, Ferriter, Jakicic, Kramer, Schuhl, Kanold, Barnes, Toncheff, Marzano, Buffum, Malone, Strong, Vagle, Marzano CEU Course on Formative Assessments, Global PD videos, Stronge and Associates, and Global PD Mini-Course on CFA

Step 5: Review, reflect, and agree on shared commitments.

	Common Formative Assessment Team Commitments
Yes, I commit	**Team Member Commitments**
	We agree that the common formative assessment measures grade-level learning for all students.
	We agree that the common formative assessment meets the success criteria listed on page —
	We agree that the common formative assessment created is both reliable and viable.
	We agree to implement the assessment on the same date and time. Date of CFA: Times:
	We agree to give the same directions to our students before the CFA.
	We agree to allow the following amount of time for the assessment:
	We agree to supply the following materials for the students:
	We agree that all students will take the CFA in the classroom.
	We agree on the following scoring plan for the CFA________________ with mastery level ____________________.

	We agree to collaboratively score the assessment with our team on the following dates ______________________ in the following location________________.
	We agree or disagree to allow students to self-grade their assessments.
	We agree that all students have the opportunity to retake the assessment.
	We agree to the following timeline of the common formative assessments: • Assessment Development: • Administration of the CFA Window: • Date to Collaboratively Score: • Scoring Completion: • Data Action Meeting: • Flex Time on the following day: • Instructional Adjustments Implemented:

Phase 3: Classroom Instruction

Ensuring High Quality Instruction in all Classrooms

6 Action Steps for a successful meeting focused on instruction:

Step 1: Begin by greeting one another, conducting a check-in, revisiting established norms, and discussing desired outcomes.

Step 2: Read, reflect, and review the Teacher Framework multiple times.

Step 3: Reflect on and discuss areas for improvement in your teaching practices using the Teacher Framework Success Criteria.

Step 4: Create and display the proficiency scales in your classroom, observe exemplary scales in other classrooms, and consult the Proficiency Scales guide.

Step 5: Engage in instructional rounds by visiting other classrooms to enhance your instructional methods.

Step 6: Ensuring high-quality instruction on a daily basis by creating instructional action plans and using proficiency scales is quality professional learning. In addition, organize your professional development to align with improving instruction.

Ensuring Effective Instruction in Every Classroom

Purpose: This section is designed for staff to meet as teams or individually to reflect on and improve classroom instruction. The goal is for every staff member to embrace continuous growth as a relentless learner and effective teacher.

Directions: Teachers read and reread the framework, then take notes in *the Reflection on Teaching section*. Teachers consider their current level of instruction, identify an area for growth, and create an action plan to improve your practice.

This phase draws heavily on the work of Robert Marzano's New Art and Science of Teaching and the PLC Framework from Solution Tree - Bo Ryan

Step 1: Greetings

Accountability Log		
Dates Met/Times	**Location Met**	**Staff Present at Meeting**

Greeting/Check-In	Norms Review	Roles	Outcome

Step 2: Read, reflect, and review the Teacher Framework multiple times.

Classroom Learning Environment	Got It!	Possible Area of Focus
Classroom Arrangement: The classroom is neat, safe, and well-organized.		
Standard Wall: The standards wall has the learning targets posted for the month written as student friendly learning goals with clear expectations for grade-level work.		
Do-Now: A brief activity is posted on standard wall or power point.		
Behavior Expectations: Behavior expectations are posted in the room.		
Word Walls: The wall shares high frequency words, words commonly misspelled in students' work, and academic vocabulary words.		
Exemplars: Samples of work that aligns with mastery of the grade-level standard.		
Classroom Library: The library is attractive, well-designed, and organized. The library has a variety of interesting books and short texts at different levels with new books displayed throughout the room. Books are easily accessible to students.		
Student Recognition: Teacher highlights student work and accomplishments of the students in the room.		
Student Supports: Create and use anchor charts, hint walls, and reminders in the room to guide students during independent practice.		
Celebrate Students: Teachers regularly recognize and celebrate students' growth and effort.		

Instruction: Do Now	Got It!	Possible Area of Focus
Do-Now: The Do-Now should only last 5-7 minutes.		
Knowledge: The Do-Now is time to activate or check prior knowledge, build background knowledge, and review vocabulary relevant to lesson.		
Pre-Assessment: Short, quick pre-assessments can be used to determine needs and gaps in students' learning.		

Instruction: Mini-Lesson	Got It!	Possible Area of Focus
Teacher Clarity: Teacher clearly states the learning target at the beginning of the lesson, states the rationale, and gives clear descriptions of what strong work looks like. Students must be able to answer 3 questions: 1) What am I learning today? 2) Why am I learning this? 3) How will I know if I learned it?		
Teacher Clarity: Teacher helps the students understand the learning targets by showing student work and examining exemplars, helping students apply clear descriptions of what strong work looks like, and providing feedback focused on the learning targets.		
Knowledge: Teacher activates or checks prior knowledge, builds background knowledge, and reviews vocabulary relevant to lesson. Note: this part of the lesson can take place as the Do-Now. Pre-assessment allows the teacher to determine what to teach, who to teach, and how to teach to promote learning.		
Explicit Teaching: Teacher thoroughly explains, demonstrates, and models the skill. The teacher connects new learning to previous learning targets, reviews information, previews and interacts with new knowledge, reviews foundational skills and vocabulary, and chunks content into small segments.		
Anchor Charts: Teacher creates anchor charts on chart paper or whiteboard in order to capture key points of the mini-lesson.		
Active Engagement: Teacher builds in many opportunities for all students to respond: whiteboards, choral responses, hand signals, numbered heads, turn and talk, and pair shares.		
Data- Driven: Teacher makes an immediate adjustment to the lesson based on student responses and evidence of learning.		
Engagement Practices: Teacher engages the students with evidence of teacher planning for engagement: pacing, teacher enthusiasm for the content, teacher passion for teaching, teacher energy, and/or student note-taking, pair shares, and discussion.		

Student Evidence (*students can*): Show evidence from Do-Now, explain the learning target and why it is important, discuss in pairs, take notes, formulate questions, initiate other students in the discussion, challenge each other's thinking, make contributions to the discussion, and justify and explain their answers.		
End of Mini-Lesson: Teacher reviews various supports for students in the room and clearly communicates expectations for practice. The teacher reviews transition procedures, the learning target, key teaching points, and the importance of the lesson.		

Instruction: Practice (small groups and independent learning)	Got It!	Possible Area of Focus
Smooth Transition: Transition from whole group to small group occurs smoothly with little to no loss of instructional time with the students assuming the responsibility.		
Time: Teacher maximizes instructional time with efficient classroom procedures and routines. Materials are prepared in advance and ready for the students.		
Learning Target: Teacher reinforces learning target throughout the lesson, links target to assignment or task, and uses the target to monitor learning. Feedback is aligned to the learning target.		
Engagement Practices: Teacher plans for engagement with small groups and independent work well-organized. There is evidence of clear, precise expectations for seat work (posted and reviewed), teacher circulating, and teacher reinforces effort and provides recognition. The teacher notices and reacts when the students are not engaged, increases students' opportunity to respond, maintains a lively pace, and keeps an eye on all students at all times.		
Learning Tasks or Assignments: The assignment or task is aligned to the grade level priority standards. The tasks involve thinking, problem-solving, reading, writing, and discussing.		
Instructional Resources & Materials: Teacher provides support for students during independent work: graphic organizers, sentence frames, notebooks, manipulatives, rubrics, computers, and anchor charts.		
Extending Thinking: Teacher provides activities and resources to extend student learning while providing students with resources and guidance.		
Collaboration: Students work in pairs or groups to engage in discussions and problem solving, use each other as academic resources, and communicate using academic language and vocabulary,		

Assessment for Learning: The teacher monitors all students, and regularly conferences or interviews with students to check on their learning and offer feedback.		
Questioning: Teacher asks high-quality questions that are prepared in advance, aligned to the learning targets, and cause all students to think and reflect. The teacher allows wait time (wait time 1) after asking a question and wait time (wait time 2) after the student answers the question.		
Student Evidence (*students can*): Students explain what they are doing, why, and what success looks like; work on challenging assignments aligned to the target; use scaffolds, answer text-dependent questions, and use evidence from text.		

Instruction: Closure with Evidence of Learning	Got It!	Possible Area of Focus
Sharing of Work: Students share their work with the teacher or their peers.		
Feedback: Teachers and peers provide specific, timely feedback to students that are aligned to the expectations of quality work.		
Self-Assessment: Students interpret scores with learning targets, track and monitor progress, self-reflect on process and effort, and set learning goals.		
Celebration: Teachers and students celebrate high-quality work and growth.		

Step 3: Reflect on, Discuss, and Create Action Plan

Read Teacher Framework, Take Notes, and Reflect on Practice
Teacher Select an Area of Focus To Improve Learning
Circle one Environment   Do-Now   Mini-Lesson   Deliberate Practice   Closure with Evidence
Teacher Action Plan: Area of Focus, Success Criteria Indicator, and Plan
Evidence of Practice and Reflections

Step 4: Post the proficiency scales within the classroom, visit other rooms to see exemplary scales, and review Proficiency Scales guide.

This framework adapts ideas from Robert Marzano's research and Marzano Resources publications

Learning Block Plan -The Team Meeting to the Classroom

Tasks to be Completed	Check
Teachers discuss and select priority standards for the upcoming learning block.	
Learning targets are formulated based on the deconstructed standards.	
Learning targets break down the priority standard into manageable segments of information.	
The teacher evaluates the cognitive demand associated with each learning target.	
The established learning target signifies mastery of the learning standard.	
The teacher creates approaching standard learning targets, which clearly articulate the prerequisite skills and vocabulary needed to master the standard. Teachers must teach the guaranteed vocabulary.	
The teacher creates a plan to push students' thinking beyond mastery of the standard.	

Proficiency Scales in the Classroom	
Adult Actions	**Check**
The standards wall is organized, clearly articulated, consistently located, and accessible to students.	
Mastery is defined as the grade-level expectation.	
Mastery is the learning target created from the priority standard.	
Mastery of the standard is expressed through student friendly learning goals displayed on the standards wall	
Clear descriptions of what strong work looks like are available for students.	
Approaching the standard includes the prerequisite skills and vocabulary aligned with the mastery of the standard. Both must be taught.	
Beyond the Standard involves thinking that goes beyond the standard, articulated in student friendly learning goals	

Using the Proficiency Scales as an Instructional Tool	
Adult and Student Actions	**Check**
Teacher Action: The teacher reviews learning targets and clear descriptions of what strong work looks like at the start, during, and conclusion of the lesson.	
Teacher Action: Feedback from the teacher is aligned with the learning targets.	
Teacher Actions: Formative assessments are aligned with the learning targets.	
Student Action: Students can articulate the learning targets.	
Student Action: Students can explain how the task aligns to the learning targets.	
Student Action: Students use the descriptions of what strong work looks like to assess their learning.	
Student Action: Students set goals and track progress.	
Student Action: Students understand their current level of performance.	
Student Action: Students and staff celebrate their success and their growth.	

Step 5: Engage in instructional rounds by visiting other classrooms to enhance your instructional methods.

Instructional Rounds Agenda

Outcome: Observe classrooms, discuss, and reflect on practice.	Norms: • Maximize time. • Respect others. • Refrain from conversations with other observers. Refrain from interrupting the lesson. • Collect factual evidence. • Do not share evidence of observation outside the team.
Pre-Rounds Collaborative Meeting	Introduce the team. Read and discuss to build shared knowledge. Discuss the rounds documents. Review norms.
Rounds in the classroom	Adhere to the norms. Read, respond, and take notes.
Post-rounds collaborative meeting in the hallway	Discuss observed strengths. Reflect on instructional practice: Which parts of your teaching do you feel good about after visiting the classroom?

<table>
<tr><td></td><td>What new ideas do you have after visiting the classroom?</td></tr>
<tr><td colspan="2">Notes:</td></tr>
</table>

Bo Ryan

Collaborative Instructional Rounds Template

Grade-Level Team:	Date of Instructional Rounds:
Facilitator:	Time:

Norms for Instructional Rounds:

• Refrain from conversations with other observers.

• Refrain from interrupting the lesson.

• Collect factual evidence.

• Do not share evidence of observation outside the team.

Focus of the Instructional Round: Proficiency Scales and Instruction

Evidence Collected:

Strengths Observed (factual):	One or Two Positives for a Sticky Note:

Teacher Reflection Questions:

Which parts of my teaching do I feel good about after visiting the classroom?	What new ideas do I have after visiting the classroom?

Phase 4: Data Action

Reflecting and Taking Action based on the Data

8 steps for having a successful meeting about taking Data Action

Step 1: Begin with greetings, conduct a check-in, and then set expectations and guidelines.

Step 2: Review the priority standards and the Common Formative Assessment (CFA).

Step 3: Analyze the data.

Step 4: Reflect on the findings from the data.

Step 5: Conduct a fidelity check to see if the team committed to the instructional plan.

Step 6: Create a plan for additional time and support.

Step 7: Organize a celebration for both students and staff.

Step 8: Taking data action is exemplary professional learning. In addition, arrange for professional development opportunities focused on data.

<u>Data Action</u>: Use the Data to Take Action

<u>Purpose</u>: In a healthy school culture, staff must know the current level of all students in order to make changes focused on student learning.

<u>Directions</u>: The data action process is for all certified teachers in the school at all grade levels: grade-level teams, subject-specific teams, singleton teachers, and humanities teachers. All staff must have a system to monitor student learning on a regular basis. Staff use the allotted time during the day to create, administer, and score common formative assessments. Teams then follow the steps in this tool to monitor student learning and to create a plan to support growth in all students.

Step 1: Greetings

Accountability Log		
Dates Met/Times	**Location Met**	**Staff Present**

Greeting/Check-In	Norms Review	Roles	Outcome

Step 2: Review Priority Standards and CFA

Priority Standards and Guaranteed Vocabulary taught during Learning Cycle
Describe Common Formative Assessment or Performance Assessment with Standard

Step 3: Review Data

Teacher's names	Number of Students who took the Assessment	Number of students at Mastery or Above	Number of students Not There Yet	Percentage of students at mastery or higher
Total:				
Data Story: Discuss student growth (pre, mid, post). Reflect on staff and student attendance.				

Step 4: Reflect on the Data

<table>
<tr><td>Data Reflection: What adjustments do we need to make in our practices to respond to these results for all students? Please include a reflection on the reliability and validity of common formative assessments, classroom instruction, and a plan for more time, support, and enrichment.</td></tr>
<tr><td> </td></tr>
<tr><td>What is your strategic plan to address achievement disparities between our student groups, especially our poor and minority students?</td></tr>
<tr><td> </td></tr>
<tr><td>What are the names of these students who are not at mastery?</td></tr>
<tr><td> </td></tr>
</table>

Step 5: Fidelity Check: Reflect on your practices

Reflect on your Learning Plan and Conduct a Fidelity Check					
Did ALL students have access to Grade-Level Instruction?	Did you use the data to reflect on and make changes to your instruction?	Did staff follow the plan for more time and support?	Did staff administer a reliable and valid Pre-CFA?	Did staff administer a reliable and valid MID-CFA?	Did you meet with your team on a regular basis?
Yes No	Yes No	Yes No	Yes No	Yes No	Yes No

Step 6: Plan for More Time and Support

Plan for Flex Block			
Date of Flex Block	Whole Class Review of Assessment	Plan for Students who did **not** learn	Plan for Students who **did** learn

Plan for More Time and Support with Team			
Date of Team Meeting	Staff in Attendance	Plan for Students who need more time and support	Plan for students who need enrichment and extension

Step 7: Plan for Celebrations

Celebrations based on the Data		
Students Growth	Students Mastery	Teammate of the Cycle

Revised from Ryan, B (2023). Brilliance in the building: Effecting change in urban schools using the PLC process. Solution tree.

Phase 5: Next Steps for Continuous Learning

Continuous Learning Plan Aligned to our Learning Cycles

Purpose: Select professional learning that is job-embedded, research-based, reflective, goal of teaching others, individual, and subject-specific.

Directions: Staff, based on where they are currently in the cycle, select their own professional learning. Staff also select professional learning based on student data.

Planning: Ensure a Guaranteed and Viable Curriculum				
Continue to Work on Learning Plan		Collaborate on lesson plans.		Create Proficiency Scales
Create a plan for more time and support.		Create exemplars, models, or worked examples of grade-level assignments.		Prepare small group instruction.
Prepare sentence starters for writing and discussions.		Create Anchor Charts		Create Word Wall and Vocabulary Wall
Study the curriculum		Create Scaffolds		Create a well-organized learning environment.
Instruction: Ensuring High-Quality Instruction				
Set, review, and reflect on Instructional Goals with Teacher Framework.		Create Proficiency Scales in the Classroom and observe other proficiency scales in other classrooms.		Use Avanti - a tool for new staff.

Video the lesson for you to observe and reflect on the instruction		Conduct Instructional Rounds		Ensure students have the tools to self-grade, chart progress, and celebrate success.	
Collaborate to create behavior-specific lessons.		Use AI to create student tasks that align with standards.		Work with a colleague to give feedback or to visit the classroom to share with you.	
Monitor Learning: Common Formative Assessment					
Create Common Formative Assessments		Create Pre/Mid/End Common Formative Assessments.		Create Assessments aligned to proficiency scales.	
Review and reread the Common Formative Assessment Tool.		Collaboratively score not only CFAs but also writing assignments.		Share work samples with your team.	
Data Action: End-of-Block Data team					
End of Learning Block Data Meeting		Create extension plans		Create Flex Block Plan	
College Prep Progress Monitoring.		Create plans for more time and support.		Reflect on other data sources.	

Reflection on time spent reading, writing, and discussing.		Quick Data Team Process.		Prepare for student retake.	
Continuous Learning for ALL: Support Staff					
Create SPED Plans		Analyze Time		Call as many families as possible for positive reasons.	
Collaborate with others focused on learning.		Prep SPED PPT.		Work on SPED BIPS/FBAs/504s.	
Book Study with Action Focus.		Read educational magazines or books.		Utilize a PLC Resource Center.	
Teach Others: Become an Expert					
Write a blog		Conduct Action Research:		Create a video documenting your success to share with others.	
Arrange room for Instructional Fairs.		Arrange the room for the instructional round visit.		Create a model classroom and invite visitors.	
Create a short podcast.		Share Student Learning Samples		Assist other teams and teachers with the process.	
Earn HRT: High Reliability Teaching Certificate and		Become an assessment expert and share with others.		Become an instructional Goal-Setting Expert.	

coaching others.			
Become a data expert and share the process with others.	Become an expert at writing IEPs and share with others.		Offer support to new teachers.
Share your professional learning with others.	Become an expert on the state testing format and test-specific questions and share with others.		Become a subject-specific expert and share with others.

Summary of your Learning for the Learning Cycle

Staff Meetings or Professional Learning Sessions Outside the School Day or ½ days	
Vertical Team Meetings (start and end of cycles)	
Professional Development Choice - collaborative or individual	
Teach Others	

Staff Celebrations	
	174
Staff Created Professional Development	
Action Plan based on options above	

Learning Block 4

Dates	
SMART Goal	

Phase 1: Planning

Ensure a Guaranteed and Viable Curriculum

8 Action Steps for a successful learning plan meeting:

Step 1: Begin by greeting one another, conducting a check-in, revisiting established norms, and discussing desired outcomes.

Step 2: Examine the curriculum in detail.

Step 3: Engage in discussions to review and prioritize standards.

Step 4: Develop proficiency scales for sharing within the classroom.

Step 5: Outline the pacing for the unit.

Step 6: Formulate an instructional plan.

Step 7: Plan for additional time and support.

Step 8: Collaboratively planning a block of time is exemplary professional learning. In addition, organize your professional development to align with the planning.

Learning Plan

Purpose: Allow staff members to plan to create a guaranteed and viable curriculum, which ensures that all students have access to the curriculum and the time to learn it. Educational researcher and author Dr. Robert Marzano states that it is the number one factor impacting student learning.

Directions: The learning plan is for all certified teachers in the school in all grade levels: grade-level teams, subject-specific teams, singleton teachers, and humanities teachers. Staff use the allotted time during the day to study and take notes on the curriculum, review priority standards, create mastery models of expected student work, create a pacing guide, and create an instructional plan. This is also a tool that can be used by coaches to guide teachers and offer support. The teacher leads this process.

Step 1: Greetings

Accountability Log		
Dates Met/Times	**Location Met**	**Staff Present at Meeting**

Greeting/Check-In	Norms Review	Roles	Outcome

Step 2: Curriculum

Study the Curriculum Materials and Take Notes

Step 2: Curriculum

Study the Curriculum Materials and Take Notes

Step 3: Discuss and Review Priority Standards

<table>
<tr><td colspan="2">List Priority Standards for Cycle of Learning with GUARANTEED Vocabulary that must be taught (post in room)</td></tr>
<tr><td>Priority Standards</td><td>Guaranteed Vocabulary</td></tr>
<tr><td></td><td></td></tr>
<tr><td colspan="2">Learning Targets Created from the Standard(s)</td></tr>
<tr><td colspan="2"></td></tr>
</table>

Process for Creating Proficiency Scales to ensure guaranteed and viable curriculum:

1) Write the learning target for mastery of standards

2) Write success criteria for mastery: what does good work look like with mastery models

3) Determine vocabulary, teach vocabulary simpler procedures, and prerequisite content

4) Discuss thinking beyond mastery with examples of exceeding

5) Discuss scaffolds for each target and teaching tips

Step 4: Create Learning Progression and Proficiency Scales

Learning Target	Approaching Standard Prerequisite Skills Guaranteed Vocabulary	Mastery of Standard w/Success Criteria	Exceeding Standard Thinking beyond mastery	Scaffolds for the Learning Targets & Teaching Tips for Exceeding Assignments
LT1				
Mastery Model, Exemplary, or Worked Example of Learning Target				
LT2				
Mastery Model, Exemplary, or Worked Example of Learning Target				
LT3				
Mastery Model, Exemplary, or Worked Example of Learning Target				
LT4				
Mastery Model, Exemplary, or Worked Example of Learning Target				

Step 5: Create Pacing for the Block

- **Examine** the curriculum, district assessment calendar, and overall district calendar.

- **Outline the schedule** for teaching learning targets, conducting common formative assessments, and allocating time for data monitoring and reflection.

- **Designate specific days** for teaching particular standards and strategize on how to assess learning through common formative assessments.

- **Identify anticipated team meeting days** and ensure alignment of professional development with these plans: review and develop the learning cycle plan, create and implement common formative assessments, analyze and reflect on the data, and formulate a data-driven action plan.

- **This collaborative strategy must be mutually agreed upon** and adhered to by the team. If they cannot, they follow the curriculum as closely as possible or ask an instructional coach for additional support and expertise.

Bo Ryan

Focus:			Number of Days:	

Pacing of Cycle from ____________ to ____________

Monday	Tuesday	Wednesday	Thursday	Friday

Step 6: Create an Instructional Plan

Instructional Plan
<ul><li>How will you ensure <u>ALL</u> students have access to grade-level assignments?</li><li>How will your team enrich and extend the learning of students beyond mastery?</li><li>What teaching practices work best for this specific priority standard?</li><li>Plan small-group instruction and/or conferences for students not at mastery.</li></ul> Small Group Math   Small Group Literacy

Step 7: Create a Plan for More Time and Support:

<table>
<tr><td colspan="3" align="center">Systematic Plan for More Time and Support</td></tr>
<tr><td align="center">Focus</td><td align="center">Teaching Plan</td><td align="center">Monitor Progress</td></tr>
<tr><td>More Time and Support on grade-level priority standards</td><td></td><td></td></tr>
<tr><td>More time and Support on Prerequisite Skills are needed to master grade-level standards</td><td></td><td></td></tr>
<tr><td>Fluency Repeated Reading Program</td><td></td><td></td></tr>
<tr><td>Enrichment</td><td></td><td></td></tr>
<tr><td>IEP Plans</td><td></td><td></td></tr>
<tr><td>Arts</td><td></td><td></td></tr>
<tr><td colspan="3" align="center">Action Plan</td></tr>
<tr><td colspan="3"></td></tr>
</table>

Revised from Ryan, B (2023). Brilliance in the building: Effecting change in urban schools using the PLC process. Solution tree.

Phase 2: Measuring Learning

Creating, Administering, and Scoring Common Formative Assessments

6 steps for having a successful meeting about common formative assessments:

Step 1: Begin by greeting one another, conducting a check-in, revisiting established norms, and discussing desired outcomes.

Step 2: Examine the criteria for developing common formative assessments (CFAs)

Step 3: Develop a CFA(s).

Step 4: Consider the reliability and validity of the CFA.

Step 5: Review, reflect, and agree on shared commitments.

Step 6: Creating common formative assessments is considered exemplary professional learning. In addition, organize a professional learning plan aligned to assessments.

Measuring Learning with Common Formative Assessments

Purpose: The purpose of the grade-level common formative assessment is to measure student learning of the guaranteed and viable curriculum. This tool gives all stakeholders shared knowledge of how to create a reliable and valid common formative assessment. The entire staff can use this in order to create common formative assessments.

Directions: Review the criteria below to support your creation of common formative assessments or performance assessments.

Step 1: Greetings

Accountability Log		
Dates Met/Times	**Location Met**	**Staff Present**

Greeting/Check-In	Norms Review	Roles	Outcome

Step 2: Examine the criteria for developing common formative assessments (CFAs)

Check	Success Criteria for an Exemplary Common Formative Assessment
	The team/teacher discusses and identifies priority standard (s) to be measured.
	The team/teacher writes the assessment around a priority standard.
	The team/teacher evaluates the depth of knowledge level (DOK) of the target(s), selects the best strategy for assessing the target (selected response, constructed response, a combination, or performance task), and aligns the assessment to the rigor of the standard.
	The team/teacher creates the assessment items that match the level of thinking of the target (determine DOK level and align to the level of demand of the question).
	The team/teacher agrees on what mastery will look like for the priority standards and the overall assessment with clear success criteria.
	The team/teacher identifies the academic language and vocabulary that need to be targeted.
	The team ensures the CFA meets the criteria: 1- 2 constructed responses, 2-4 selected responses, or a combination of both per assessment.
	The team/teacher creates an assessment that is neat, organized, and easy to read with adequate space to write and solve problems. The directions and questions are clearly written. The learning target(s) are written on the assessment.
	The team/teacher creates an assessment that is quick to administer, appropriate for the time allotted, and easy to score.
	The students must be a part of the assessment process: clarity on mastery of the standard, review of the assessment, opportunity to retake, and time in the schedule for flex time for reteaching from the teacher. Students set goals and celebrate growth.

Bo Ryan

Success Criteria for an Exemplary Performance Assessment	
	The team/teacher determines the focus of the performance assessment.
	The team/teacher makes sure the assessment aligns with the priority standard.
	The team/teacher is clear about what the students must demonstrate for mastery.
	The team/teacher creates success criteria to describe the expectations of mastery.
	The team/teacher assesses the students by observation or examining a product.
	The team/teacher will share examples of the performance assessment.

Revised from Ryan, B (2023). Brilliance in the building: Effecting change in urban schools using the PLC process. Solution tree.

Step 3: Develop a CFA.

<u>Common Formative Assessment Framework Model</u>

Student Name:	**Date:**	Grade:

Name of CFA:

<u>**Standard:**</u>

<u>**Precise Directions for CFA**</u>:

<u>**Questions Aligned to LT**</u>

Review the Learning Plan and Share Links of your Common Formative Assessments for this Cycle			
Pre-CFA	Mid-CFA	Additional CFA	End-CFA

Step 4: Review Common Formative Assessments and Formative Assessments for Reliability and Validity

The essence of assessments lies in ensuring they are both reliable and valid.

- **Validity:** This refers to the extent to which an assessment accurately measures what the team believes students should have learned, ensuring alignment with instructional goals.

- **Reliability:** This indicates that students who demonstrate understanding of the concepts have genuinely grasped them.

Three Intentional Steps for Developing Valid and Reliable Assessments:

- Identify the learning target.

- Determine the level of rigor of the target.

- Decide on the types and quantity of items for the assessment.

Evaluating the Quality of an Assessment

Is it VALID?

We have pinpointed specific learning targets.

We have established the rigor level for each target.

The assessment items correspond to the cognitive demands of the learning targets.

Is it RELIABLE?

We utilized a sufficient number of questions to ensure reliability.

The team has reached a consensus on the criteria for mastery.

The reading levels of the questions do not hinder the assessment.

Adapted from the work of Ainsworth, Bailey, Erkens, Ferriter, Jakicic, Kramer, Schuhl, Kanold, Barnes, Toncheff, Marzano, Buffum, Malone, Strong, Vagle, Marzano CEU Course on Formative Assessments, Global PD videos, Stronge and Associates, and Global PD Mini-Course on CFA

Step 5: Review, reflect, and agree on shared commitments.

Common Formative Assessment Team Commitments	
Yes, I commit	**Team Member Commitments**
	We agree that the common formative assessment measures grade-level learning for all students.
	We agree that the common formative assessment meets the success criteria listed on page —
	We agree that the common formative assessment created is both reliable and viable.
	We agree to implement the assessment on the same date and time. Date of CFA: Times:
	We agree to give the same directions to our students before the CFA.
	We agree to allow the following amount of time for the assessment:
	We agree to supply the following materials for the students:
	We agree that all students will take the CFA in the classroom.
	We agree on the following scoring plan for the CFA________________ with mastery level __________________.

	We agree to collaboratively score the assessment with our team on the following dates ___________________ in the following location_______________.
	We agree or disagree to allow students to self-grade their assessments.
	We agree that all students have the opportunity to retake the assessment.
	We agree to the following timeline of the common formative assessments: • Assessment Development: • Administration of the CFA Window: • Date to Collaboratively Score: • Scoring Completion: • Data Action Meeting: • Flex Time on the following day: • Instructional Adjustments Implemented:

Phase 3: Classroom Instruction

Ensuring High Quality Instruction in all Classrooms

6 Action Steps for a successful meeting focused on instruction:

Step 1: Begin by greeting one another, conducting a check-in, revisiting established norms, and discussing desired outcomes.

Step 2: Read, reflect, and review the Teacher Framework multiple times.

Step 3: Reflect on and discuss areas for improvement in your teaching practices using the Teacher Framework Success Criteria.

Step 4: Create and display the proficiency scales in your classroom, observe exemplary scales in other classrooms, and consult the Proficiency Scales guide.

Step 5: Engage in instructional rounds by visiting other classrooms to enhance your instructional methods.

Step 6: Ensuring high-quality instruction on a daily basis by creating instructional action plans and using proficiency scales is quality professional learning. In addition, organize your professional development to align with improving instruction.

Ensuring Effective Instruction in Every Classroom

Purpose: This section is designed for staff to meet as teams or individually to reflect on and improve classroom instruction. The goal is for every staff member to embrace continuous growth as a relentless learner and effective teacher.

Directions: Teachers read and reread the framework, then take notes in *the Reflection on Teaching section*. Teachers consider their current level of instruction, identify an area for growth, and create an action plan to improve your practice.

This phase draws heavily on the work of Robert Marzano's New Art and Science of Teaching and the PLC Framework from Solution Tree - Bo Ryan

Step 1: Greetings

Accountability Log		
Dates Met/Times	**Location Met**	**Staff Present at Meeting**

Greeting/Check-In	Norms Review	Roles	Outcome

Step 2: Read, reflect, and review the Teacher Framework multiple times.

Classroom Learning Environment	Got It!	Possible Area of Focus
Classroom Arrangement: The classroom is neat, safe, and well-organized.		
Standard Wall: The standards wall has the learning targets posted for the month written as student friendly learning goals with clear expectations for grade-level work.		
Do-Now: A brief activity is posted on standard wall or power point.		
Behavior Expectations: Behavior expectations are posted in the room.		
Word Walls: The wall shares high frequency words, words commonly misspelled in students' work, and academic vocabulary words.		
Exemplars: Samples of work that aligns with mastery of the grade-level standard.		
Classroom Library: The library is attractive, well-designed, and organized. The library has a variety of interesting books and short texts at different levels with new books displayed throughout the room. Books are easily accessible to students.		
Student Recognition: Teacher highlights student work and accomplishments of the students in the room.		
Student Supports: Create and use anchor charts, hint walls, and reminders in the room to guide students during independent practice.		
Celebrate Students: Teachers regularly recognize and celebrate students' growth and effort.		

Instruction: Do Now	Got It!	Possible Area of Focus
Do-Now: The Do-Now should only last 5-7 minutes.		
Knowledge: The Do-Now is time to activate or check prior knowledge, build background knowledge, and review vocabulary relevant to lesson.		
Pre-Assessment: Short, quick pre-assessments can be used to determine needs and gaps in students' learning.		

Instruction: Mini-Lesson	Got It!	Possible Area of Focus
Teacher Clarity: Teacher clearly states the learning target at the beginning of the lesson, states the rationale, and gives clear descriptions of what strong work looks like. Students must be able to answer 3 questions: 1) What am I learning today? 2) Why am I learning this? 3) How will I know if I learned it?		
Teacher Clarity: Teacher helps the students understand the learning targets by showing student work and examining exemplars, helping students apply clear descriptions of what strong work looks like, and providing feedback focused on the learning targets.		
Knowledge: Teacher activates or checks prior knowledge, builds background knowledge, and reviews vocabulary relevant to lesson. Note: this part of the lesson can take place as the Do-Now. Pre-assessment allows the teacher to determine what to teach, who to teach, and how to teach to promote learning.		
Explicit Teaching: Teacher thoroughly explains, demonstrates, and models the skill. The teacher connects new learning to previous learning targets, reviews information, previews and interacts with new knowledge, reviews foundational skills and vocabulary, and chunks content into small segments.		
Anchor Charts: Teacher creates anchor charts on chart paper or whiteboard in order to capture key points of the mini-lesson.		
Active Engagement: Teacher builds in many opportunities for all students to respond: whiteboards, choral responses, hand signals, numbered heads, turn and talk, and pair shares.		
Data- Driven: Teacher makes an immediate adjustment to the lesson based on student responses and evidence of learning.		
Engagement Practices: Teacher engages the students with evidence of teacher planning for engagement: pacing, teacher enthusiasm for the content, teacher passion for teaching, teacher energy, and/or student note-taking, pair shares, and discussion.		

Student Evidence (*students can*): Show evidence from Do-Now, explain the learning target and why it is important, discuss in pairs, take notes, formulate questions, initiate other students in the discussion, challenge each other's thinking, make contributions to the discussion, and justify and explain their answers.		
End of Mini-Lesson: Teacher reviews various supports for students in the room and clearly communicates expectations for practice. The teacher reviews transition procedures, the learning target, key teaching points, and the importance of the lesson.		

Instruction: Practice (small groups and independent learning)	Got It!	Possible Area of Focus
Smooth Transition: Transition from whole group to small group occurs smoothly with little to no loss of instructional time with the students assuming the responsibility.		
Time: Teacher maximizes instructional time with efficient classroom procedures and routines. Materials are prepared in advance and ready for the students.		
Learning Target: Teacher reinforces learning target throughout the lesson, links target to assignment or task, and uses the target to monitor learning. Feedback is aligned to the learning target.		
Engagement Practices: Teacher plans for engagement with small groups and independent work well-organized. There is evidence of clear, precise expectations for seat work (posted and reviewed), teacher circulating, and teacher reinforces effort and provides recognition. The teacher notices and reacts when the students are not engaged, increases students' opportunity to respond, maintains a lively pace, and keeps an eye on all students at all times.		
Learning Tasks or Assignments: The assignment or task is aligned to the grade level priority standards. The tasks involve thinking, problem-solving, reading, writing, and discussing.		
Instructional Resources & Materials: Teacher provides support for students during independent work: graphic organizers, sentence frames, notebooks, manipulatives, rubrics, computers, and anchor charts.		
Extending Thinking: Teacher provides activities and resources to extend student learning while providing students with resources and guidance.		
Collaboration: Students work in pairs or groups to engage in discussions and problem solving, use each other as academic resources, and communicate using academic language and vocabulary,		

Assessment for Learning: The teacher monitors all students, and regularly conferences or interviews with students to check on their learning and offer feedback.		
Questioning: Teacher asks high-quality questions that are prepared in advance, aligned to the learning targets, and cause all students to think and reflect. The teacher allows wait time (wait time 1) after asking a question and wait time (wait time 2) after the student answers the question.		
Student Evidence (*students can*): Students explain what they are doing, why, and what success looks like; work on challenging assignments aligned to the target; use scaffolds, answer text-dependent questions, and use evidence from text.		

Instruction: Closure with Evidence of Learning	Got It!	Possible Area of Focus
Sharing of Work: Students share their work with the teacher or their peers.		
Feedback: Teachers and peers provide specific, timely feedback to students that are aligned to the expectations of quality work.		
Self-Assessment: Students interpret scores with learning targets, track and monitor progress, self-reflect on process and effort, and set learning goals.		
Celebration: Teachers and students celebrate high-quality work and growth.		

Step 3: Reflect on, Discuss, and Create Action Plan

<table>
<tr><td>Read Teacher Framework, Take Notes, and Reflect on Practice</td></tr>
<tr><td></td></tr>
<tr><td>Teacher Select an Area of Focus To Improve Learning</td></tr>
<tr><td>Circle one

Environment   Do-Now   Mini-Lesson   Deliberate Practice   Closure with Evidence</td></tr>
<tr><td>Teacher Action Plan: Area of Focus, Success Criteria Indicator, and Plan</td></tr>
<tr><td></td></tr>
<tr><td>Evidence of Practice and Reflections</td></tr>
<tr><td></td></tr>
</table>

Step 4: Post the proficiency scales within the classroom, visit other rooms to see exemplary scales, and review Proficiency Scales guide.

This framework adapts ideas from Robert Marzano's research and Marzano Resources publications

Learning Block Plan -The Team Meeting to the Classroom	
Tasks to be Completed	**Check**
Teachers discuss and select priority standards for the upcoming learning block.	
Learning targets are formulated based on the deconstructed standards.	
Learning targets break down the priority standard into manageable segments of information.	
The teacher evaluates the cognitive demand associated with each learning target.	
The established learning target signifies mastery of the learning standard.	
The teacher creates approaching standard learning targets, which clearly articulate the prerequisite skills and vocabulary needed to master the standard. Teachers must teach the guaranteed vocabulary.	
The teacher creates a plan to push students' thinking beyond mastery of the standard.	

Proficiency Scales in the Classroom	
Adult Actions	**Check**
The standards wall is organized, clearly articulated, consistently located, and accessible to students.	
Mastery is defined as the grade-level expectation.	
Mastery is the learning target created from the priority standard.	
Mastery of the standard is expressed through student friendly learning goals displayed on the standards wall	
Clear descriptions of what strong work looks like are available for students.	
Approaching the standard includes the prerequisite skills and vocabulary aligned with the mastery of the standard. Both must be taught.	
Beyond the Standard involves thinking that goes beyond the standard, articulated in student friendly learning goals	

Using the Proficiency Scales as an Instructional Tool	
Adult and Student Actions	**Check**
Teacher Action: The teacher reviews learning targets and clear descriptions of what strong work looks like at the start, during, and conclusion of the lesson.	
Teacher Action: Feedback from the teacher is aligned with the learning targets.	
Teacher Actions: Formative assessments are aligned with the learning targets.	
Student Action: Students can articulate the learning targets.	
Student Action: Students can explain how the task aligns to the learning targets.	
Student Action: Students use the descriptions of what strong work looks like to assess their learning.	
Student Action: Students set goals and track progress.	
Student Action: Students understand their current level of performance.	
Student Action: Students and staff celebrate their success and their growth.	

Step 5: Engage in instructional rounds by visiting other classrooms to enhance your instructional methods.

Instructional Rounds Agenda

Outcome: Observe classrooms, discuss, and reflect on practice.	Norms: • Maximize time. • Respect others. • Refrain from conversations with other observers. Refrain from interrupting the lesson. • Collect factual evidence. • Do not share evidence of observation outside the team.
Pre-Rounds Collaborative Meeting	Introduce the team. Read and discuss to build shared knowledge. Discuss the rounds documents. Review norms.
Rounds in the classroom	Adhere to the norms. Read, respond, and take notes.
Post-rounds collaborative meeting in the hallway	Discuss observed strengths. Reflect on instructional practice: Which parts of your teaching do you feel good about after visiting the classroom?

<table>
<tr><td></td><td>What new ideas do you have after visiting the classroom?</td></tr>
<tr><td colspan="2">Notes:</td></tr>
</table>

Collaborative Instructional Rounds Template

Grade-Level Team:	Date of Instructional Rounds:
Facilitator:	Time:

Norms for Instructional Rounds:

• Refrain from conversations with other observers.

• Refrain from interrupting the lesson.

• Collect factual evidence.

• Do not share evidence of observation outside the team.

Focus of the Instructional Round: Proficiency Scales and Instruction

Evidence Collected:

Strengths Observed (factual):	One or Two Positives for a Sticky Note:

Teacher Reflection Questions:

Which parts of my teaching do I feel good about after visiting the classroom?	What new ideas do I have after visiting the classroom?

Phase 4: Data Action

Reflecting and Taking Action based on the Data

8 steps for having a successful meeting about taking Data Action

Step 1: Begin with greetings, conduct a check-in, and then set expectations and guidelines.

Step 2: Review the priority standards and the Common Formative Assessment (CFA).

Step 3: Analyze the data.

Step 4: Reflect on the findings from the data.

Step 5: Conduct a fidelity check to see if the team committed to the instructional plan.

Step 6: Create a plan for additional time and support.

Step 7: Organize a celebration for both students and staff.

Step 8: Taking data action is exemplary professional learning. In addition, arrange for professional development opportunities focused on data.

<u>Data Action</u>: Use the Data to Take Action

<u>Purpose</u>: In a healthy school culture, staff must know the current level of all students in order to make changes focused on student learning.

<u>Directions</u>: The data action process is for all certified teachers in the school at all grade levels: grade-level teams, subject-specific teams, singleton teachers, and humanities teachers. All staff must have a system to monitor student learning on a regular basis. Staff use the allotted time during the day to create, administer, and score common formative assessments. Teams then follow the steps in this tool to monitor student learning and to create a plan to support growth in all students.

Step 1: Greetings

Accountability Log		
Dates Met/Times	**Location Met**	**Staff Present**

Greeting/Check-In	Norms Review	Roles	Outcome

Step 2: Review Priority Standards and CFA

Priority Standards and Guaranteed Vocabulary taught during Learning Cycle
Describe Common Formative Assessment or Performance Assessment with Standard

Step 3: Review Data

Teacher's names	Number of Students who took the Assessment	Number of students at Mastery or Above	Number of students Not There Yet	Percentage of students at mastery or higher
Total:				
Data Story: Discuss student growth (pre, mid, post). Reflect on staff and student attendance.				

Step 4: Reflect on the Data

<table>
<tr><td>Data Reflection: What adjustments do we need to make in our practices to respond to these results for all students? Please include a reflection on the reliability and validity of common formative assessments, classroom instruction, and a plan for more time, support, and enrichment.</td></tr>
<tr><td>

</td></tr>
<tr><td>What is your strategic plan to address achievement disparities between our student groups, especially our poor and minority students?</td></tr>
<tr><td>

</td></tr>
<tr><td>What are the names of these students who are not at mastery?</td></tr>
<tr><td>

</td></tr>
</table>

Step 5: Fidelity Check: Reflect on your practices

Reflect on your Learning Plan and Conduct a Fidelity Check					
Did ALL students have access to Grade-Level Instruction?	Did you use the data to reflect on and make changes to your instruction?	Did staff follow the plan for more time and support?	Did staff administer a reliable and valid Pre-CFA?	Did staff administer a reliable and valid MID-CFA?	Did you meet with your team on a regular basis?
Yes No	Yes No	Yes No	Yes No	Yes No	Yes No

Step 6: Plan for More Time and Support

Plan for Flex Block			
Date of Flex Block	Whole Class Review of Assessment	Plan for Students who did **not** learn	Plan for Students who **did** learn

Plan for More Time and Support with Team			
Date of Team Meeting	Staff in Attendance	Plan for Students who need more time and support	Plan for students who need enrichment and extension

Step 7: Plan for Celebrations

Celebrations based on the Data		
Students Growth	Students Mastery	Teammate of the Cycle

Revised from Ryan, B (2023). Brilliance in the building: Effecting change in urban schools using the PLC process. Solution tree.

Phase 5: Next Steps for Continuous Learning

Continuous Learning Plan Aligned to our Learning Cycles

Purpose: Select professional learning that is job-embedded, research-based, reflective, goal of teaching others, individual, and subject-specific.

Directions: Staff, based on where they are currently in the cycle, select their own professional learning. Staff also select professional learning based on student data.

Planning: Ensure a Guaranteed and Viable Curriculum					
Continue to Work on Learning Plan		Collaborate on lesson plans.		Create Proficiency Scales	
Create a plan for more time and support.		Create exemplars, models, or worked examples of grade-level assignments.		Prepare small group instruction.	
Prepare sentence starters for writing and discussions.		Create Anchor Charts		Create Word Wall and Vocabulary Wall	
Study the curriculum		Create Scaffolds		Create a well-organized learning environment.	
Instruction: Ensuring High-Quality Instruction					
Set, review, and reflect on Instructional Goals with Teacher Framework.		Create Proficiency Scales in the Classroom and observe other proficiency scales in other classrooms.		Use Avanti - a tool for new staff.	

Video the lesson for you to observe and reflect on the instruction		Conduct Instructional Rounds		Ensure students have the tools to self-grade, chart progress, and celebrate success.	
Collaborate to create behavior-specific lessons.		Use AI to create student tasks that align with standards.		Work with a colleague to give feedback or to visit the classroom to share with you.	

Monitor Learning: Common Formative Assessment

Create Common Formative Assessments		Create Pre/Mid/End Common Formative Assessments.		Create Assessments aligned to proficiency scales.	
Review and reread the Common Formative Assessment Tool.		Collaboratively score not only CFAs but also writing assignments.		Share work samples with your team.	

Data Action: End-of-Block Data team

End of Learning Block Data Meeting		Create extension plans		Create Flex Block Plan	
College Prep Progress Monitoring.		Create plans for more time and support.		Reflect on other data sources.	

Reflection on time spent reading, writing, and discussing.		Quick Data Team Process.		Prepare for student retake.	
Continuous Learning for ALL: Support Staff					
Create SPED Plans		Analyze Time		Call as many families as possible for positive reasons.	
Collaborate with others focused on learning.		Prep SPED PPT.		Work on SPED BIPS/FBAs/504s.	
Book Study with Action Focus.		Read educational magazines or books.		Utilize a PLC Resource Center.	
Teach Others: Become an Expert					
Write a blog		Conduct Action Research:		Create a video documenting your success to share with others.	
Arrange room for Instructional Fairs.		Arrange the room for the instructional round visit.		Create a model classroom and invite visitors.	
Create a short podcast.		Share Student Learning Samples		Assist other teams and teachers with the process.	
Earn HRT: High Reliability Teaching Certificate and		Become an assessment expert and share with others.		Become an instructional Goal-Setting Expert.	

coaching others.					
Become a data expert and share the process with others.		Become an expert at writing IEPs and share with others.		Offer support to new teachers.	
Share your professional learning with others.		Become an expert on the state testing format and test-specific questions and share with others.		Become a subject-specific expert and share with others.	

Summary of your Learning for the Learning Cycle

Staff Meetings or Professional Learning Sessions Outside the School Day or ½ days	
Vertical Team Meetings (start and end of cycles)	
Professional Development Choice - collaborative or individual	
Teach Others	

Staff Celebrations	222
Staff Created Professional Development	
Action Plan based on options above	

Part 3: Professional Learning at the End of the Year

All of these tools can be used by teachers and staff during their end-of-school-year professional development days.

End-of-Year Flashback Data Reflection on Priority Standards

Purpose: The purpose of this tool is to review the priority standards students struggled with during the year to focus on the standard, not the student. Great tool to use at the end of the school year. This aligns with the start of the year, focus on priority standards.

Directions: Please list below 3 priority standards that gave your students the most challenges during the last school year. Please write the standard in the box below. In addition, please list when the standard was taught during the year. Lastly, list the data source that was used. If possible, attach the common formative assessment that is aligned with the standard. The goal is to create a plan at the vertical team level.

Accountability Log		
Dates Met/Times	**Location Met**	**Staff Present at Meeting**

Greeting/Check-In	Norms Review	Roles	Outcome

Questions for Discussion and Notes Section

1) **Content Teachers:**

    a) What were the challenges with this standard?

    b) What do you suggest stopping doing?

    c) What strategy worked really well with this standard?

    d) Can you share mastery models and exemplars that align with the standard?

e) What are the immediate prerequisite skills that must be taught at the beginning of a unit?

f) What scaffolds were successful in helping ALL students access grade-level curriculum?

g) Can you attach your common formative assessment to this document?

h) Other thoughts…

Immediate Thoughts and Reflections

Subject:

Priority Standard	What cycle was this taught in?	What cycle did you revisit?	How did you measure learning?

Notes:

Priority Standard	What cycle was this taught in?	What cycle did you revisit?	How did you measure learning?

Notes:

Priority Standard	What cycle was this taught in?	What cycle did you revisit?	How did you measure learning?

Notes:

Data Action Plan: Review at the end of the Year

Purpose: The purpose of this tool is for either the school-wide leadership team or the grade level teams to share data from the learning cycle, highlight a challenge or success, and take an action step.

Directions: The teacher leaders review the academic data. This plan can be led by a leadership team or grade-level team. Someone on the team, like the administration, should have the behavior and attendance data ready for the meeting. Time is a data source to use to reflect on student absences, staff absences, the number of students late to class, assemblies, and other school-wide issues that impact time on instruction. The team selects

Action Plan					
Date/Time/ Attendance	Greetings	Norms	Roles	Cycle	Team
				Cycle 1 Cycle 2 Cycle 3 Cycle 4	Grade-Level Leadership Team District

Collaborative Action Plan Tool

	Academics	Behavior	Attendance	Time	Other Data
Data					
Challenge/Success based on the data					
1 Action Step					
Celebrations					
Individual Students who need support					
Leadership Support					

<u>Purpose</u>: The purpose of this tool is for either the school-wide leadership team or the grade level teams to rate, reflect, and create a plan at the end of the year for each phase

<u>Directions</u>: The teacher leaders review the chart below. This plan can be led by a leadership team or grade-level team. The leaders evaluate themselves as either mastery, next level, or needs support. Staff who rate themselves as Next Level must have evidence for the rating.

Professional Learning: Team Action Plan	Team Rating		
<u>Phase 1: Planning</u>: Teams establish and implement a guaranteed and viable curriculum, unit by unit, that ensures that all students have access to the grade-level priority standards regardless of their assigned teacher.	**Next Level**	**Mastery**	**Needs Support**
Evidence and Action Plan			
<u>Phase 2: Monitoring Learning:</u> Teams monitor student learning through an assessment process that includes daily checks for understanding, formative assessments aligned to learning targets, and team-created common formative assessments.	**Next Level**	**Mastery**	**Needs Support**
Evidence and Action Plan			
<u>Phase 3: Instruction:</u> Teams ensure high-quality instruction in all classrooms focused on instructional goal setting, reflection, using proficiency scales, and instructional rounds.			
<u>Phase 4: Data Action:</u> Teams meet to analyze the results from team-created common formative assessments to reflect on and	**Next**	**Mastery**	**Needs**

improve teacher practice, build collective efficacy, and intervene, enrich, or extend student learning.	**Level**		**Support**
Evidence and Action Plan			
Phase 5: Continuous Learning: Teachers will continuously improve their practice during the school year by creating professional learning sessions that meet their needs.	**Next Level**	**Mastery**	**Needs Support**
Evidence and Action Plan			

See free reproducibles from the book, Brilliance in the Building: https://www.solutiontree.com/free-resources/plcbooks/bib to support your work.

<u>11</u> Core Values Focused on Student Learning, Culture, and Equity

<u>**Purpose**</u>: The purpose of this tool is for all staff to make the connection between culture, equity, and student learning.

<u>**Directions:**</u> The Staff reads the 11 core values, discusses as a team, and reviews how they keep each other accountable for following the core values.

1) Collaborative meetings are student-centered and focused on equity.

2) We will have an unwavering commitment to student achievement using the cycles of learning.

3) We will ensure all students have access to grade-level standards in all classes.

4) We will refrain from using negative comments or excuses about students in meetings.

5) We will make data-driven changes to our practices and policies.

6) We will monitor student data and participate in aligned professional development in order to impact student learning.

7) We will highlight, publicize, and celebrate the achievements of our staff and students.

8) We will expect that what we do will impact student learning.

9) If disparities exist between student groups, especially poor and minority students, we will implement a strategic plan, and there is longitudinal evidence that the gaps are closing.

10) If we identify and recognize student gaps in the areas of background knowledge and academic skill, we will create and implement a plan to address these issues, and we have evidence of longitudinal growth.

11) We will use practices most likely to make an impact on student learning.

Epilogue

I am so excited to get this book out in print. I have been working on this book for over 20 years. Leaders can take this book and begin the process of improving schools immediately, not because schools need to be fixed, but because we can do even better. Put the teachers in charge, maximize time during the day, ensure their success in meetings, and offer a variety of professional learning options, and watch the school soar! Professional learning is a process. The learning block cycle is professional learning at its best! It connects staff learning to daily practice. This book will directly improve classroom instruction and student learning!

Additional Resources:

Ainsworth, L. (2015a). Common formative assessments 2.0: How teacher teams intentionally align standards, instruction, and assessment. Thousand Oaks, CA: Corwin.

Ainsworth, L. (2015b). Unwrapping the Common Core: A practical process to manage rigorous standards. Englewood, CO: Lead and Learn Press.

Almarode, J. T., Fisher, D., Thunder, K., & Frey, N. (2021). The success criteria playbook: A hands-on guide to making learning visible and measurable, grades K–12. Thousand Oaks, CA: Corwin.

Bailey, K., & Jakicic, C. (2017). Simplifying common assessment: A guide for Professional Learning Communities at Work. Bloomington, IN: Solution Tree Press.

Bailey, K., & Jakicic, C. (2019). Make it happen: Coaching with the four critical questions of PLCs at Work. Bloomington, IN: Solution Tree Press.

Bailey, K., & Jakicic, C. (2021). The collaborative team plan book for a PLC at Work. Bloomington, IN: Solution Tree Press.

Bailey, K., Jakicic, C., DuFour, R., DuFour, R., Keating, J., Kramer, S. V., et al. (2019). Common formative assessment [Video course]. Bloomington, IN: Solution Tree Press.

Bailey, K., Jakicic, C., & Spiller, J. (2014). Collaborating for success with the Common Core: A toolkit for Professional Learning Communities at Work. Bloomington, IN: Solution Tree Press.

Borrero, K. K. (2019). Every student, every day: A No-Nonsense Nurturer approach to reaching all learners. Bloomington, IN: Solution Tree Press.

Buffum, A., Mattos, M., & Malone, J. (2025). Taking action: A handbook for RTI at Work. Second Edition. Bloomington, IN: Solution Tree Press.

Buffum, A., & Mattos, M. (2020). RTI at Work plan book. Bloomington, IN: Solution Tree Press.

Buffum, A., Mattos, M., & Malone, J. (2018). Taking action: A handbook for RTI at Work. Bloomington, IN: Solution Tree Press.

Buffum, A., Mattos, M., & Weber, C. (2012). Simplifying response to intervention: Four essential guiding principles. Bloomington, IN: Solution Tree Press.

Depka, E. (2017). Raising the rigor: Effective questioning strategies and techniques for the classroom. Bloomington, IN: Solution Tree Press.

Dimich, N. (2015). Design in five: Essential phases to create engaging assessment practice. Bloomington, IN: Solution Tree Press.

Donohoo, J. (2017). Collective efficacy: How educators' beliefs impact student learning. Thousand Oaks, CA: Corwin.

DuFour, R. (2015). In praise of American educators: And how they can become even better. Bloomington, IN: Solution Tree Press.

DuFour, R. (2017a, Fall). First thing: Answer why before what and how. AllThingsPLC Magazine, 4–5.

DuFour, R. (2017b, Summer). Pursuing attainable and stretch goals in a PLC. AllThingsPLC Magazine, 36–37.

DuFour, R., & DuFour, R. (2012). The school leader's guide to Professional Learning Communities at Work. Bloomington, IN: Solution Tree Press.

DuFour, R., DuFour, R., & Eaker, R. (2006). Professional Learning Communities at Work plan book. Bloomington, IN: Solution Tree Press.

DuFour, R., DuFour, R., & Eaker, R. (2008). Revisiting Professional Learning Communities at Work. New insights for improving schools (1st ed.). Bloomington, IN: Solution Tree Press.

DuFour, R., DuFour, R., Eaker, R., & Karhanek, G. (2004). Whatever it takes: How professional learning communities respond when kids don't learn. Bloomington, IN: Solution Tree Press.

DuFour, R., DuFour, R., Eaker, R., & Karhanek, G. (2010). Raising the bar and closing the gap: Whatever it takes. Bloomington, IN: Solution Tree Press.

DuFour, R., DuFour, R., Eaker, R., & Many, T. (2006). Learning by doing: A handbook for Professional Learning Communities at Work (1st ed.). Bloomington, IN: Solution Tree Press.

DuFour, R., DuFour, R., Eaker, R., & Many, T. (2010). Learning by doing: A handbook for Professional Learning Communities at Work (2nd ed.). Bloomington, IN: Solution Tree Press.

DuFour, R., DuFour, R., Eaker, R., Many, T. W., & Mattos, M. (2016). Learning by doing: A handbook for Professional Learning Communities at Work (3rd ed.). Bloomington, IN: Solution Tree Press.

DuFour, R., DuFour, R., Eaker, R., Mattos, M., & Muhammad, A. (2021). Revisiting Professional Learning Communities at Work: Proven insights for sustained, substantive school improvement (2nd ed.). Bloomington, IN: Solution Tree Press.

DuFour, R., DuFour, R., Eaker, R., Many, T., Mattos, M., & Muhammad, A. (2024). Learning by doing: a handbook for professional learning communities at work. (4th ed.). Bloomington, IN: Solution Tree Press.

DuFour, R., & Eaker, R. (1987). Fulfilling the promise of excellence: A practitioner's guide to school improvement. Westbury, NY: Wilkerson.

DuFour, R., & Eaker, R. (1992). Creating the new American school: A principal's guide to school improvement. Bloomington, IN: National Educational Service.

DuFour, R., & Eaker, R. (1998). Professional Learning Communities at Work: Best practices for enhancing student achievement. Bloomington, IN: Solution Tree Press.

DuFour, R., Eaker, R., & DuFour, R. (Eds.). (2005). On common ground: The power of professional learning communities. Bloomington, IN: Solution Tree Press.

DuFour, R., & Fullan, M. (2013). Cultures built to last: Systemic PLCs at Work. Bloomington, IN: Solution Tree Press.

DuFour, R., & Marzano, R. J. (2011). Leaders of learning: How district, school, and classroom leaders improve student achievement. Bloomington, IN: Solution Tree Press.

DuFour, R., & Reason, C. (2016). Professional Learning Communities at Work and virtual collaboration: On the tipping point of transformation. Bloomington, IN: Solution Tree Press.

DuFour, R., Reeves, D., & DuFour, R. (2018). Responding to the Every Student Succeeds Act with the PLC at Work process. Bloomington, IN: Solution Tree Press.

Eaker, R. (2020). A summing up: Teaching and learning in effective schools and PLCs at Work. Bloomington, IN: Solution Tree Press.

Eaker, R., DuFour, R., & DuFour, R. (2002). Getting started: Reculturing schools to become professional learning communities. Bloomington, IN: Solution Tree Press.

Eaker, R., & Keating, J. (2015). Kid by kid, skill by skill: Teaching in a Professional Learning Community at Work. Bloomington, IN: Solution Tree Press.

Eaker, R., & Marzano, R. J. (Eds.). (2020). Professional Learning Communities at Work and High Reliability Schools: Cultures of continuous learning. Bloomington, IN: Solution Tree Press.

Erkens, C. (2016). Collaborative common assessments: Teamwork. Instruction. Results. Bloomington, IN: Solution Tree Press.

Erkens, C. (2019). The handbook for collaborative common assessments: Tools for design, delivery, and data analysis. Bloomington, IN: Solution Tree Press.

Fisher, D., Frey, N., Amador, O., & Assof, J. (2019). The teacher clarity playbook: A hands-on guide to creating learning intentions and success criteria for organized, effective instruction, grades K–12. Thousand Oaks, CA: Corwin.

Fleischman, S. (2005, March 1). Research matters: Positive culture in urban schools. ASCD. Accessed at https://ascd.org/el/articles/positive-culture-in-urban-schools on April 7, 2022.

Frey, N., Hattie, J., & Fisher, D. (2018). Developing assessment-capable visible learners, grades K–12: Maximizing skill, will, and thrill. Thousand Oaks, CA: Corwin.

Friziellie, H., Schmidt, J. A., & Spiller, J. (2025). All means all: Essential actions for leveraging yes we can. Bloomington, IN: Solution Tree Press.

Friziellie, H., Schmidt, J. A., & Spiller, J. (2016). Yes we can! General and special educators collaborating in a professional learning community. Bloomington, IN: Solution Tree Press.

Hall, B. (2022). Powerful guiding coalitions: How to build and sustain the leadership team in your PLC at Work. Bloomington, IN: Solution Tree Press.

Hannigan, J., Hannigan, J. D., Mattos, M., & Buffum, A. (2021). Behavior solutions: Teaching academic and social skills through RTI at Work. Bloomington, IN: Solution Tree Press.

Hansforn, N. (2025). The scientific principles of teaching: Bringing the devide between educational practice and research. Bloomington, IN: Solution Tree Press.

Hattie, J. (2015, June). What works best in education: The politics of collaborative expertise. London: Pearson. Accessed at www.pearson.com/content/dam/corporate/global/pearson-dot-com/files/hattie/150526 _ExpertiseWEB_V1.pdf on September 30, 2015.

Hattie, J., Fisher, D., & Frey, N. (2017). Visible learning for mathematics, grades K–12: What works best to optimize student learning. Thousand Oaks, CA: Corwin.

Hattie, J., & Smith, R. (Eds.). (2021). Ten mindframes for leaders: The visible learning approach to school success. Thousand Oaks, CA: Corwin.

Hattie, J., & Zierer, K. (2018). Ten mindframes for visible learning: Teaching for success. New York: Routledge.

Hirsh, S., & Crow, T. (2017). Becoming a learning team: A guide to teacher-led cycle of continuous improvement. Oxford, OH: Learning Forward.

Hoegh, J. K. (2020a). A handbook for developing and using proficiency scales in the classroom. Bloomington, IN: Marzano Resources.

Hoegh, J. K. (2020b). Six action steps for a guaranteed and viable curriculum. In R. Eaker & R. J. Marzano (Eds.) Professional Learning Communities at Work and High Reliability Schools: Cultures of continuous learning (pp. 129–146). Bloomington, IN: Solution Tree Press

Kramer, S. V. (2015). How to leverage PLCs for school improvement. Bloomington, IN: Solution Tree Press.

Kramer, S. V. (Ed.). (2021). Charting the course for collaborative teams: Lessons from priority schools in a PLC at Work. Bloomington, IN: Solution Tree Press.

Kramer, S. V., & Schuhl, S. (2017). School improvement for all: A how-to guide for doing the right work. Bloomington, IN: Solution Tree Press.

Learning Forward (2011). Standards for professional learning: Quick reference guide. Accessed at https://ndlegis.gov/assembly/62-2011/docs/pdf/eft021612appendixf.pdf on April 21, 2022.

Many, T. W., Maffoni, M. J., Sparks, S. K., & Thomas, T. F. (2018). Amplify your impact: Coaching collaborative teams in PLCs at Work. Bloomington, IN: Solution Tree Press.

Many, T, W., Maffoni, M. J., Sparks, S. K., & Thomas, T. F. (2020). How schools thrive: Building a coaching culture for collaborative teams in PLCs at Work. Bloomington, IN: Solution Tree Press.

Many, T. W., Maffoni, M. J., Sparks, S. K., & Thomas, T. F. (2022). Energize your teams: Powerful tools for coaching collaborative teams in PLCs at Work. Bloomington, IN: Solution Tree Press.

Many, T. W., & Sparks-Many, S. K. (2015). Leverage: Using PLCs to promote lasting improvement in schools. Thousand Oaks, CA: Corwin.

Marzano, R. J. (2011, February 1). The art and science of teaching: Making the most of instructional rounds. ASCD. Accessed at https://ascd.org/el/articles/making-the-most-of-instructional-rounds on December 2, 2021.

Marzano, R. J. (2017). The new art and science of teaching. Bloomington, IN: Solution Tree Press.

Marzano, R. J. (2018). The new art and science of teaching [Video]. Bloomington, IN: Solution Tree Press.

Marzano, R. J., Frontier, T., & Livingston, D. (2011). Effective supervision: Supporting the art and science of teaching. Alexandria, VA: Association for Supervision and Curriculum Development.

Marzano, R. J., Heflebower, T., Hoegh, J. K., Warrick, P. B., & Grift, G. (2016). Collaborative teams that transform schools: The next step in PLCs. Bloomington, IN: Marzano Resources.

Marzano, R. J., & Marzano, J. S. (2003). The key to classroom management. Educational Leadership, 61(1), 6–13.

Marzano, R. J., Pickering, D. J., & Pollack, J. E. (2001). Classroom instruction that works: Research-based strategies for increasing student achievement. Alexandria, VA: Association for Supervision and Curriculum Development.

Marzano, R. J., Warrick, P. B., Rains, C. L., & DuFour, R. (2018). Leading a High Reliability School. Bloomington, IN: Solution Tree Press.

Mattos, M., & Buffum, A. (Eds.). (2015). It's about time: Planning interventions and extensions in secondary school. Bloomington, IN: Solution Tree Press.

Mattos, M., DuFour, R., DuFour, R., Eaker, R., & Many, T. W. (2016). Concise answers to frequently asked questions about Professional Learning Communities at Work. Bloomington, IN: Solution Tree Press.

Muhammed, A. (2015). Overcoming the achievement gap trap: Liberating mindsets to effect change. Bloomington, IN: Solution Tree Press.

Muhammad, A. (2018). Transforming school culture: How to overcome staff division (2nd ed). Bloomington, IN: Solution Tree Press.

Reeves, D. (2020a). Achieving equity and excellence: Immediate results from the lessons of high-poverty, high-success schools. Bloomington, IN: Solution Tree Press.

Reeves, D. B. (2020b). The learning leader: How to focus improvement for better results (2nd ed.). Alexandria, VA: Association for Supervision and Curriculum Development.

Reeves, D., & DuFour, R. (2016). The futility of PLC lite. Phi Delta Kappan, 97(6), 69–71.

Reeves, D., & Eaker, R. (2019). 100-day leaders: Turning short-term wins into long-term success in schools. Bloomington, IN: Solution Tree Press.

Rogers, P., Smith, W. R., Buffum, A., & Mattos, M. (2021). Best practices at Tier 3: Intensive interventions for remediation, secondary. Bloomington, IN: Solution Tree Press.

Schmoker, M. (2006). Results now: How we can achieve unprecedented improvements in teaching and learning. Alexandria, VA: Association for Supervision and Curriculum Development.

Schmoker, M. (2011). Focus: Elevating the essentials to radically improve student learning (1st ed.). Alexandria, VA: Association for Supervision and Curriculum Development.

Schmoker, M. (2018). Focus: Elevating the essentials to radically improve student learning (2nd ed.). Alexandria, VA: Association for Supervision and Curriculum Development.

Sonju, B., Kramer, S. V., Mattos, M., & Buffum, A. (2019). Best practices at Tier 2: Supplemental interventions for additional student support, secondary. Bloomington, IN: Solution Tree Press.

Spiller, J., & Power, K. (2019). Leading with intention: Eight areas for reflection and planning in your PLC at Work. Bloomington, IN: Solution Tree Press.

Stronge, J. H., Grant, L. W., & Xu, X. (2017). Designing effective assessments. Bloomington, IN: Solution Tree Press.

\